A LIFE WORTH TAKING

C. G. COOPER

"A LIFE WORTH TAKING"

Book 1 of the Tom Greer novels
Copyright © 2018 C. G. Cooper Entertainment, LLC.
All Rights Reserved
Author: C. G. Cooper

**Get a FREE copy of *Adrift*, the first book in the Daniel Briggs
spinoff, just for subscribing at http://CG-Cooper.com**

PROLOGUE

I *don't want to die anymore.*
There, I said it.

Want me to say it again? Okay, fine.

Just kidding. I won't. I don't like repeating myself anyway. Don't make me. It wouldn't be good.

I rise off the soiled couch cushion that feels like a melted marshmallow. It's hard not to notice these things now. When I walked into the room, nothing had registered. Not the sights. Not the smells.

Not the danger.

But now I see it all. Everything.

I inhale deeply. Ages of cigarette tar. Asbestos-filled walls that would make a building inspector cringe. Spoiled milk, or is that something even worse? The place definitely needs a thorough cleaning.

Not that it matters.

I pick up the gallon-sized gas can and twist off the cap. I'm not even shaking. A minute later, the contents of said container are scattered around the room. Quick work. Too easy.

I inhale again. The smell of gas masks everything, and I like it. It smells like freedom - burning, biting, powerful freedom.

Think on it later, I tell myself. *Steep in it like tea. There's a job to do.*

The lighter appears from my pocket like a magic trick. I have a way of letting it slip out into my palm from behind my fingers as if it's materializing out of nothing. I learned it years ago to impress women. Now it's a habit, and I do it even when I'm alone.

With flick of my thumb the flame licks out. Hungry. Ready.

I watch as it sways in the dead air, at one point threatening to die out. It rages back to life, hungrier still. I can't help but feel a kinship.

"It's all yours, brother," I say to the flame, kneeling down to touch it to the gas-soaked carpet.

With a muted *fwoomp*, the dingy space blooms to flame, my little brother doing my bidding. He follows my primer trail, engulfing one human foot, and then another, where they lie pointed up at the ceiling a few yards away. Searing tendrils lick their way up legs, a torso, and finally, across the familiar face.

No screams. No terror. It's too late for that.

"See ya around," I say, pausing long enough to spit on the roasting corpse one last time.

My flame brother never touches me, never doles out the pain it should.

I smile, tip my head to the inferno, and then leave with my freedom.

It's gonna be a great day.

A DAY IN THE LIFE

"**A**re you going to fly our plane?"

The confident young voice cut through my daydreaming. Another one about the flame.

I looked down at the little girl with twin hair braids wearing a yellow sundress. Her eyes twinkled with curiosity and an utter lack of fear. Lucky girl.

I smiled.

"I sure am," I said, handing my credentials to the airline attendant.

"Thank you, Captain," said the woman with a smile and a glance toward the little girl.

"Are you any good at flying airplanes?" the girl persisted.

"I am," I replied.

"Well, that's good. I need to get home to see Tiger." She shifted her backpack from one shoulder to the other. She couldn't be more than five years old.

"Who's Tiger?" I heard myself ask.

"My dog."

"Oh? What kind of dog?"

"A mastiff."

I let out a low whistle. "Big dog."

The young girl nodded, barely hiding the fact that she already knew the dog was big, and that I might be a passable listener. Ah, the confidence of youth.

"He sleeps with me. I take care of him."

Just then, a harried man with a cell phone pasted to his ear showed up. He wore a rumpled suit and a crust of what I hoped was donut glaze in the corner of his mouth.

"Don't bother the flight attendant, Jenny," the man said, reaching for the little girl's arm without removing the phone from his ear. I didn't like his tone. Something in me bristled.

Jenny swerved deftly. Obviously not her first time dodging her father. I liked this girl.

"I'm not bothering him, Daddy." Then she turned to me. "I thought you were flying the plane."

Something changed in the father's face, as if reality had just slapped him in the fraction of a moment. "Oh, I'm sorry. I didn't see your, um, uniform."

Hard to miss with the coat and funny cap, jackass.

"Jenny was just telling me about Tiger," I said.

"What? Oh yeah, Tiger." His focus popped back to the device in hand. He intoned something official and commanding into his phone before regarding me again with what I can only describe as dismissive attention. "Anyway, Captain..." He squinted, looking for a name tag.

"Stubing, and this is my Love Plane," I answered, still smiling. The cultural ignoramus didn't get my joke. "Just kidding. It's Greer."

Jenny didn't give daddy a chance to recover. "Nice to meet you, Mr. Greer," she said, sticking out a hand.

Her grasp was firm, and she looked straight into my eyes - no fear. I wondered where she picked that up. Definitely not her father, who looked closer and closer to a panic attack as he struggled to keep the cell to his ear while fumbling for his boarding pass. I heard snippets of someone speaking on the other end of his phone in a staccato barrage of updates, facts, and figures.

"I think it's *Captain* Greer, honey," Jenny's father interjected. *Too little, too late, pal.*

"You can call me Tom," I said to the girl. "But your daddy has to call me Captain." I threw in a wink for good measure and she giggled.

"You're funny, Tom," she said.

"And you are welcome on my plane any time, Jenny."

She was still holding my hand at this point and wouldn't let go. Or was that me? I didn't have time to consider which before clown-box Dad cut in and grabbed his little girl's arm, pulling her away.

"I'm sorry for bothering you," he said without affect, his attention on the conference call.

Jenny waved. "See you on the plane." She beamed, nonplussed by her father's behavior. I returned the gesture, half thinking that I should snatch the girl from her inattentive father and have him banned from ever flying again.

Get with it, Tom.

"Captain?" It was the airline representative.

I turned. "Is she ready for me?"

"She is, Captain."

I touched the bill of my cap and headed down the gangplank.

My high was still with me as I mentally clocked in at work.

* * *

"Someone's in a chipper mood this morning," my co-pilot said as I stepped into the cockpit of the Boeing 777-300 - my baby for the day.

Kyle Tanner, my friend for years, was grinning like he'd had a swell night with a bevy of Bangkok madams.

"Oh?" I said. I was already in work mode, doing my pre-flight checks, inspecting my phone for any last-minute emails from corporate.

"I saw you talking to the little girl. You haven't smiled that wide since..."

I froze. Kyle was no idiot. I didn't have to tell him that his mouth had run away again. The inner bristling began again, and I tamped it down with a well-worn boot. He coughed once, his throat's way of telling his brain that it was time to move on to other subjects. I didn't look up from my phone.

"Can I get you a cup of coffee?" he asked by way of apology.

"Sure. See if they have any heavy cream. The thicker the better."

That stopped Kyle cold.

"But you like it black."

I still didn't look up. "Cream is pretty good. You should try some.

Kyle snorted. Ex-Navy fighter jocks like Kyle "Scorch" Tanner don't put cream or sugar in their coffee. It's not just a crime, but a sin. I knew what he was thinking, but he knew better than to voice it.

"Oh," I said, "and I wouldn't mind some eggs and bacon if the chef is up and running. No rush."

I was usually the one who fetched coffee and food for my team, but since Kyle had stuck his foot in his mouth...

"No problem," he said. "Anything else?"

"Nope. Thanks."

He threw me a sidelong glance that I caught out of the corner of my eye. I wondered what he must be thinking. He was probably wondering what *I* was thinking. It didn't matter. He knew better than to ask. I'm one of those guys who's known for his moods - not that my other half ever came out at work. Here, I was Captain Tom Greer, veteran pilot and all-around good guy.

Kyle closed the cockpit door behind him for some reason. It gave me a few precious moments to think about Jenny. Then my thoughts drifted to the previous night. Dark, wonderful deeds - a salve over my tender wounds. I could still smell the gasoline. I took an extra long shower to make sure I was fresh as a daisy and not reeking of my other gig. That's how I thought of it now. My *other* gig.

I settled into my routine, checking and rechecking, even though most of it is unnecessary. A bird like this one could basically fly itself. Some day, they won't need us pilots anymore, but that'll be long after I'm gone, I'm sure of it.

Long gone.

Two words with so much meaning.

When will that be me?

Not anytime soon. I was sure of that.

Buoyed by a renewed vigor and the icing of the Jenny interlude, my life felt pretty damn peachy keen, and nothing short of a crash landing into the Pacific Ocean could kill that now.

DEEP THOUGHTS WITH TOM GREER

I know what you're thinking. This guy is crazy. Straight off his rocker, two sheets to the loony bin, running around with a bloody knife and a mask on, crazy. Am I right?

Or maybe you're the more politically correct type. You've read a couple chapters and all of a sudden I'm a sociopath. Let's look at that word together, because, believe me, I've done the research.

Here's the handy definition our good friends Merriam and Webster provide for sociopath:

> **Sociopath**: *n. someone who behaves in a dangerous or violent way towards other people and does not feel guilty about such behavior*

Well, according to that definition, you could be right.

But don't you find it interesting that *you're* the one judging *me*. You don't even know me. You've read a few lines and all of a sudden we're on to the assumption game. What does that make you?

Good ol' Wikipedia came to the rescue on this one. Here's what our collective online brain says:

Jumping to conclusions: a psychological term referring to a communication obstacle where one judges or decides something without having all the facts; to reach unwarranted conclusions.

Wikipedia goes on to list three subtypes: mind reading, fortune telling, and labeling.

Can you read minds? Are you willing to tell my fortune for a couple bucks? Or is it just that you feel comfortable sticking labels on every person you meet? Is that how you deal with the world?

I won't bore you any longer. I hated it when teachers and grandparents used to lecture me on the merits of proper English. I won't apologize for stepping up onto my soapbox, but I will caution you to take a moment before shuffling me into some imaginary category. Things may not be as they seem, dear reader, and if I've offended you, feel free to stop reading.

But if you want to get to the bottom of what's really going on in my steel-trap skull, keep flipping the pages. You'll find out soon enough what makes this old crow tick.

THE INCIDENT

"There's a model in coach. A real stunner. I was thinking about upgrading her seat," Kyle said as I performed my umpteenth check of our progress.

"Do whatever you want."

"I mean it. Hottest girl I've seen since that looker in Fiji. Remember her? What was her name, Kirie, Callie...?"

"Lydia," I answered without looking up.

"Lydia! Ah, how could I forget Lydia, just like the sister in *Pride and Prejudice*."

Now I turned. "You can't remember the name of the most beautiful girl we've seen in the last five years, but you can remember the name of a supporting character in a Jane Austen novel?"

Kyle shrugged. "What? I loved that movie. The one with Keira Knightly. That Mr. Darcy was a hardass."

He'd done it. Two hours into our flight out of Thailand, and he'd finally gotten me. Ever since he stepped on his tongue, Mr. Surfer-wannabe had been trying to apologize. Kyle's way of apologizing was to distract you, to get you to forget about his indiscretion. The funny part was that I couldn't be mad at him. Ever.

Kyle's like everyone's prankster younger brother. He has a knack for getting himself into a jam, but when he finally squeezes out, he comes bearing gifts of champagne and caviar. It was no wonder there's been a steady succession of Mrs. Kyles, and that every guy wants to be his friend.

"But man, it's that Jane who really wets my whistle. What's her name? Rosamund Pike? Didn't she date Elon Musk?"

Before I could answer, there was a knock at the cabin door. I glanced at the video monitor to see that it was our head flight attendant, Gloria.

"How may I be of service?" I asked through the intercom.

"Captain, there's a situation in Business Elite."

Before you start jumping to conclusions again, "situation" does not mean a terrorist is threatening to blow us to smithereens. "Situation" is the word my team uses if there is a person who needs my personal attention.

"Good luck," Kyle said, shifting to take over management of the computer network in the sky. "Take some gloves. I'll bet it's a girl."

I didn't catch what he was referring to until I was halfway out the door. A few months before, on the Sydney to San Fran hop, a baby literally fell into my lap, covered in whatever it is newborns are covered with.

I heard Kyle's pinched balloon laugh as I closed the cabin door behind me.

"What is it, Gloria?"

Gloria was my command master chief. If I was the admiral in command, she was the one making sure the ship stayed as stable as it should be. A twenty-some-year veteran of the friendly skies, Gloria was my go-to whip cracker.

"The *gentleman*," she dragged out the word, "in Business

Elite thinks we're some kind of party barge. I've tried to talk him down, but he keeps being inappropriate with my staff."

"I'll take care of it," I said.

Before we got to the scene of the crime, I could hear bass thumping from some unseen speaker. Not one of the plane's.

Peeling back the curtain separating the elite from the uber elite, I found our culprit.

Early thirties. Half his hair styled and perfect, the other half sticking out at a right angle. He wore obnoxious over-sized sunglasses, and he was singing at the top of his lungs.

He was so into his performance that he didn't even notice when Gloria and I entered the picture. I had to give it to him. The guy could sing, although he was having a tough time with the high notes.

Other attendants – even the chef – were parked at varying intervals from our maestro, probably Gloria's doing. My people seemed calm, if not amused, except for the new girl, Faith. This was only her second run with my team. Her eyes were swollen and her carefully applied makeup was smeared.

You can mess with me all you want. Hell, mess with my plane and I won't jump down your throat in most cases. But mess with one of my people....

It took me a few seconds to find the Bluetooth speaker. I calmly held down the power button and Pavarotti's background music faded away.

"Hey!" the young man said. It was a long moment before he figured out that I was the one who'd turned it off. His eyes brightened. "There he is, the captain! Hey, Captain! I'm just trying to get the rest of these stiffs to join me for a libation."

"Sir, let's get you back to your seat and we'll talk about it there," I said. The other passengers looked up at me, almost pleading with me to put the guy in cuffs and throw him out the emergency exit. Sorry. That's not how things work.

"What? I'm not done singing." He stepped down from his

perch and staggered toward me, his cloud of booze preceding him. "How 'bout you, Cap? One for the air?" He spit-chuckled at his own lame joke.

I smiled. Yeah, it was difficult, but he was a paying customer. "I'd love to, but I'm on duty. Now, why don't you—"

"Aw man, don't be such a party pooper." He pouted like a three-year-old. I wondered how many drinks he was actually holding in the tank, or if it was just low tolerance.

"Sir, if you can please sit down, I'm sure we can make this the most comfortable flight you've ever had."

He wasn't listening. His attention was on Faith. "Hey you, why don't you come have a seat in my lap? Come on. Tell Santa what you want for Christmas." The words came out crystal clear. No slur.

"Sir..." I started to say, but suddenly he lunged for Faith, who, for some unknown reason, chose to move in closer. Maybe she thought I would need her testimony. Maybe she wanted to get a closer view of what I'd do to the idiot. Either way, she stepped too close, and suddenly he was all over her.

Faith screamed, which set off a screamfest from a particularly stalwart gaggle of ladies in aisle three.

"Come on, honey," said our gin-soaked Romeo, wrapping his arms around the unfortunate Faith.

I had enough. One hand on his shoulder was enough to tear him off Faith. He whirled on me, eyes blazing.

"Do you know who I am?" he sneered.

"Sir," I said, "if you do not comply with my commands, I will be forced to put you in restraints." My voice was eerily calm, as was the cabin, except for some sniffling in aisle three.

"Force *me?* I could buy this plane."

My tone went from calm to soothing. No need to incite a riot. "Let's talk about this at your seat."

He jabbed his finger at me. "I see what you're doing." Then he whipped around, slashing his finger at the other passengers. "Don't look at me! Don't ever look at me!" His eyes returned to me.

I was ready for the bull rush. It's happened before.

But it never came. Instead, he whipped around again and laid a flat palm across Faith's cheek, sending her crashing into the couple sitting in aisle seven.

That was the final straw.

I rushed forward and grabbed him by the neck, digging my fingers into his pressure points. There are so many all over the human body, and usually some pressure is all it takes for a rowdy partygoer to back down.

But Karaoke Josh Grobin wasn't bending. He was stronger than I thought. He turned on me, somehow sliding through my grasp. His fists were clenched, pure rage in his eyes. No talking this one down.

His hook was fast. He'd obviously had some hand-to-hand training in his life that even his inebriated state couldn't dampen. The shot would've gotten most people. Easy knock-out. Average Joe never would have seen it coming. But I did. Despite my relaxed outward appearance, I was a snake ready to strike.

So as the punch veered toward its target, aka My Melon, I bent my knees and coiled my torso to the right. Pickled Placido Domingo was too late with his correction. Like the 100+ mph swing of a PGA pro, my body uncoiled. The usual spot for the hit from my position would've been the sternum. Good shot. Nine out of ten down.

But like him or not, this was still a paying customer, and there are a variety of things that can go wrong in the human body when you get someone in the sternum.

No problem.

Input accepted.

Course correction made.

My open palm slammed into his gut, and yes, I did hear

the whoosh of the breath escaping his body.

And that was it.

Martini Casanova crumpled to the deck gasping for air that would not come.

"Get me the cuffs," I said, my voice conversational.

Gloria produced two thick zip ties and I went to work securing Andrea Bocelli's hands behind his back.

"If you're good, we'll switch these to the front in a few minutes," I said, "If you're not..."

He didn't need any further convincing. When I got him to his feet, he lolled from side to side. I prayed he wasn't going to vomit. Some people tend to do that after getting punched in the stomach. Luckily, he didn't puke and was compliant as a baby rabbit as I escorted him to his seat.

"I can take it from here, Captain," Gloria said, producing another set of zip ties and proceeding to secure the man's feet to his chair.

The entire cabin erupted in applause.

"I'm sorry for the disturbance, folks," I said. Somebody actually asked for my autograph. I smiled and went to check on Faith.

"Are you okay?"

She nodded, trying to hide her crying. She was holding the side of her face.

"Here, let me take a look."

She moved her hand, revealing an angry red mark. It was already growing into a welt which in time would become a nasty bruise. I probed the site and she winced, but took the pain like a champ.

"I don't think anything's broken," I said, "but let's have a doctor check it out when we get home, okay?" I turned back to the crew. "Any reason the rest of you can't chip in to cover Faith's post for the rest of the flight?" Head shakes all around.

"I'm okay, Captain," said Faith. Tough lady.

"Are you sure?"

She nodded confidently, her face now completely devoid of tears. And not a sniffle to be heard. "I'll just get cleaned up and it's back to work."

With the show over, my crew snapped back to routine, quickly restoring normalcy.

As for me, I didn't even make it to the curtain when a man I didn't recognize entered the my personal space.

"Can I help you?" I asked, assuming he'd heard the commotion and came to gawk. He wore a stylish button-down, and a pair of thin reading glasses were perched on top of his head.

"What happened up here?" he asked.

"Nothing we couldn't handle," I said with a professional smile. "Sorry, but if you'll excuse me, I need to get back to the cockpit."

Most people move out of the way when the person who's supposed to be flying the plane says those words. But he just stood there staring at me.

He shook his head after a few seconds, as if he'd just remembered why he'd sought me out. "Sorry. I was actually coming to find you, Captain."

I don't know why, but I didn't like the guy's tone. Offi-cious yet condescendingly friendly. Like a guy who's auditing your taxes. Why did he rankle me more than the man I just put down?

I summoned the recommended daily allowance of patience every airline pilot needs, smiled, and asked again, "How can I help you?"

It took him a long moment to respond. He was still staring at me, as if with curiosity, or was it something else?

Finally, he gave a smile and reached into his pocket. From this he produced a familiar badge.

"Ned Baxter," he said. "FBI."

BAXTER

It was a testament to my past that I did not react. Every pain and setback I'd endured had built a barrier of dead skin as thick as the Great Wall.

"Do you have a couple minutes to talk, Captain?"

"For the FBI? Of course." I positively oozed graciousness.

"I'm sorry to spring this on you."

"We play for the same team, right?"

"Of course."

"How about you give me a half hour to get cleaned up," I pointed back to the recent altercation as way of explanation, "and check to make sure we're not flying to the North Pole? Then, I'm all yours."

I said the words, but deep inside, in a place Agent Ned Baxter could never see, I was already planning.

"That would be excellent. Thank you, Captain."

"Please, call me Tom."

"Ned," Agent Baxter said, extending his hand. I shook it, feeling the strength there. He threw off the vibe of one of those bookish agents, but his grip told me something different: Ned was a person to watch.

Don't slip around this one, Tom.

Thirty minutes later, Agent Baxter and I were in the comfortable space nestled roughly above the cockpit. It afforded the space for four crew members to sleep, take a hot shower, and just get away from the constant demands of the aircraft and its passengers.

"It never ceases to amaze me the creature comforts they put in these things," Baxter said, taking it all in. "You served, right?"

Getting right down to it, eh, Agent?

"I did."

"Military service is never as glamorous as they make it look in the commercials."

I waited for him to elaborate. He didn't. I surmised this is the way he did business. Throw a statement out there, let it marinate in a suspect's brain, and then watch him squirm and spill his guts.

Did you know that the average human hates an extended lull in a conversation? It's true. Try it sometime. In the middle of your next tête-à-tête with a coworker, pause and see what happens. Some squirm and look at you funny. Others rush to fill in the gap with a joke or change the subject.

But not me. I've seen it all. Sorry, Agent Baxter.

He took his time touring the crew quarters. When he was satisfied, he returned to where I'd taken a seat, grabbing a bottle of water in the process.

"How do you do it?" Baxter asked, grabbing a seat across from me.

The soft jingling of alarm bells sounded deep inside me. "Do what, Ned?"

He gazed around the room. "Leave for days at a time. Fly around the world. Eating food out of airport restaurants and kiosks."

"It's not so bad. Pay's pretty good too."

He grinned. "I know. I checked."

What else have you checked, Agent Baxter?

It was time to use my duty card. "Listen, not for nothin', Ned, but there's work to be done. A transpacific flight does need its captain."

"Right. Sorry about that." He pulled a folded piece of paper from his pocket and took his time flattening it out. "Should've put it in an envelope," he said to no one in particular. When the single sheet was unfolded to his liking, he laid it face down on his lap. "How many oceanic trips do you take in a given year, Captain?"

"It's Tom, remember?"

"Sure."

Tough nut.

I sat back in the recliner and did the quick math, or at least I wanted him to think so. I was all about full disclosure, but if he wanted to be coy, I was fine playing along. "It depends."

"On?"

"How busy I want to be."

"So, your employer lets you set your own schedule?"

"To a certain degree. I still bid for time off, but I've been with the airline a long time. I make sure our passengers are safe, and the company takes care of me."

There was a barely perceptible tug at the corner of his mouth. I didn't like it.

"And how about that nuisance customer in Business Elite? How will the airline execs feel about that?"

Another twist. No problem.

"There'll be a debrief, of course, but it's nothing I haven't handled before."

"You did a pretty good job *handling* the singing terrorist."

So, he did see that. If he was trying to get under my skin, he was in for extreme disappointment.

I shrugged. "It happens from time to time. Usually, we can talk a person down. But if anyone lays a hand on one of my people..."

"You *handle* them."

"Sometimes."

We both let that sink in.

Baxter shook his head like he'd just remembered why he'd requested an audience with me. "I go off on tangents. It was one of the reasons my ex-wife left. She'd finally had enough of me grilling diner cooks, Uber drivers, hotel *maître d'*s. I'm curious. What can I say?"

"Curiosity killed the cat?" I said it with a smile, of course.

"More like curiosity saddled the cat with an alimony payment."

He didn't apologize. He just pressed on. I found myself admiring that fact. He gets dumped by his wife for being too curious, too full of questions, and yet, like a child who looks on the world with wonder, Agent Ned Baxter moved on.

He turned the mysterious piece of paper over in his lap. "I've been tasked by the Bureau to lead an investigation into smuggling aboard commercial airliners. Have you had any experience with this?"

"A little."

Again, the long pause. This time it felt like a welcome break in the middle of a marathon, just long enough to gather my thoughts and guess where the conversation might lead.

Baxter continued. "I've had a look at your file. On no fewer than twenty-three of your flights, personnel of varying agencies have found everything from drugs to luxury brand knockoffs."

"Only twenty-three?" I laughed. "That's not much over the course of my career."

"You don't think that's twenty-three too many?"

"It falls within the realm of acceptable losses. It's unfortunate, but it's the reality of my job."

"Those are only the ones we know of," Baxter said, not looking up from the paper. "Most of the time, someone got lucky on our end or got stupid on the criminal end." He looked up at me and stared me right in the eye. "We'd like to change that."

"And so you're here to...?"

He shrugged. "To pick your brain. Figure out how best to tackle the problem." Baxter edged forward, moving in to give me what had no doubt taken a battalion of analysts to figure out, but what we in the airline industry had probably known for decades. "They're getting smarter, Captain. Gone are the days of homemade bombs and mom and pop smuggling operations. Explosives are nearly undetectable. Special components are higher than commercial grade, not only cunning in their design, but lethal if tampered with. Certain organizations are paying a lot of money to remake the smuggling industry. I'm here as part of an international effort to stop them cold."

None of this was news to me. The booby-trapped stuff was a little high fantasy, but the rest I'd seen firsthand. Suitcases full of money. Inert explosives strapped to every body part imaginable. Live animals sedated and crammed into spaces smaller than a shoe.

But this stuff was peanuts compared to the number of goods coming into the country via shipping containers, private vessels and automobiles, and even people just strolling across the border. Smuggling anything onto a plane was a high-risk proposition. Think of all the layers of security between a foreign airport and the United States.

"There can't be that much contraband coming in," I said.

"You're right. But it isn't the amount, it's the process and goods being delivered that I've been tasked to unearth."

"Sounds like fun."

Baxter shrugged again. "It's not glamorous, I admit. But it has its perks."

"Such as?"

He handed me the crumpled piece of paper. I didn't want to take it. Something about the way he was grinning at me gave me that creeping feeling of compulsive cringing.

"You can read it, if you want," he said.

I didn't want to. Secret memos delivered at 35,000 feet were never good.

"Give me the Cliffs Notes version," I said.

"It's just an agreement between our respective employers."

"And?"

"And, I'm going to be your personal shadow for a few months."

He didn't see me shiver. That was internal, like the low rumble of a coming earthquake, the precursor to something deeper, stronger.

"My shadow?"

"You've been flying for a long time, Captain. When the FBI reached out to your bosses, you were on the top of the list of experts they recommended."

"Recommended for what, exactly?"

I had to get out of this. Things were finally going my way. How could the pinheads on the board do this to me?

"Every flight, every destination. I'll be here."

"That's a lot of time."

"It'll take as long as it takes." And he was serious. Agent Baxter was like a bloodhound hell-bent on catching its prey. This was one of those assignments given to a person who would not tire of poring through a warehouse of documents.

That's where Baxter's innate curiosity had taken him - straight to me.

"What are my responsibilities?"

"It's all there in the letter. Nothing changes except that I'll be with you. I will not get in the way of your normal duties, I promise."

"I hate to say this, Ned, but this feels like punishment. What do I need to do to get out of this chickenshit assignment? Forgive my French."

For the first time, I saw his facade waver. He didn't know how to respond. Had he expected me to jump up and down with glee at the prospect of working with a real-life FBI agent? Sorry, not sorry.

His mouth hung open for a second. "I... well..."

One point Greer.

"I'm just messing with you, Ned. In the military, we have this little running joke that you never volunteer for anything. But I guess in this case it's not really up to us, now is it?"

I chuckled. Baxter tried to match my mirth, but there was only awkward insincerity in his tone. He recovered quickly.

"I'm sorry, Captain. I take my job very seriously, sometimes to a fault."

"Ask your ex-wife?"

Now his smile was genuine. "Exactly. Now, if it's not too much trouble, I'd like to go over our schedule for the next two months."

NASHVILLE

We touched down in Nashville early afternoon the next day. I'd hitched a ride home after landing back in the States. The flight was smooth and the landing was bumpy, but I still took the time to go to the cockpit and say thanks for the ride.

I love coming home to Nashville. Its international airport is easy to navigate and, as long as you avoid the hour-long traffic in the morning and the hour-long traffic in the afternoon, the commute is never that bad. But this time I noticed that Nashville was growing. It seemed like every time I looked at downtown, there was a new high-rise building going up and a gaggle of giggling bridesmaids cruising by on their Pedal Tavern, their fake tanned legs pumping their way to the next local bar. Nashville had become a destination for bachelor and bachelorette parties. So much so that you couldn't get a hotel room downtown for less than a couple of hundred bucks a night. *Ouch*.

They said it was good for the city, good for our economy, but part of me missed the old Nashville, when I could park a block away from the honky tonk bars and sit and listen to music all night long. Now I had to compete with thousands of strangers just to breathe the hallowed air. I don't like what happens when you let time get a hold of places, let alone people.

But other than the increased hustle and bustle, Nashville's a great town. More and more, it's inhabited by transplants like me, non-natives who had moved there at some point in their lives. I had once lived outside the city in one of Nashville's suburbs, but a couple of years earlier, I'd been convinced to sell my sprawling home and elbow my way into town. Though I'd been to many of the world's largest cities, I'd never lived in one, at least not downtown.

Living a stone's throw away from the hot nightlife had come as a bit of a shock. But The Gulch had become my home. Cut just south of the train tracks bordering Nashville proper, The Gulch had once been a collection of worn-down office buildings and well-used warehouses. Now it was a mixed-use metropolis. The word "metropolis" isn't very Nashville. Then again, a lot of things in Nashville now aren't very Nashville. But condo buildings mingle perfectly with restaurants and retail. I didn't even need a car anymore. It was either walk or call for a ride.

The Uber driver who'd picked me up at the airport dropped me off in front of my condo. I slipped him a five.

"Hey, thanks. You want help with your bag?" the young man asked.

"I'm good," I said, saluting him with two fingers. "Have a great day."

He nodded, completing our transaction. In no time, I was on the top floor entering my penthouse.

Before you peg me as some highfalutin vanilla latte millionaire or something, let me tell you this: I have close to zero vices. I don't drive fancy cars. I don't take expensive vacations. My only vice is that I prefer my living space to have a decent view, and that was why I bought the penthouse suite. Yes, it was way too much room, but the view reminded me of flying. I was above the fray. Untouchable. Safe.

I thought about getting in a quick workout. I'd set up a passable home gym in one of the unused corners. Free weights, pull up bar.

Nope. That would have to wait.

I had an appointment. I showered and slipped into something casual. Thirty minutes after arriving, and just like that, I was gone again, picked up this time by a spunky coed with a Vanderbilt sticker on the back of her Hyundai. Instead of slipping in the back, I got into the passenger seat.

"Hi, Tom," she said pulling out of the loading zone like she was leaving a bank heist. She got an angry honk from a delivery van in the process.

"Yeah, your mother," she snarled.

"Slow down, Avery."

She ignored my command and zipped in and out of traffic like she was losing a tail.

"How was your trip?" she asked once we'd made it onto 12th Avenue in one piece.

"Uneventful," I said.

Avery snorted. "Yeah, right. You can tell the truth. I swept the car for bugs before I left."

I rolled my eyes but chuckled. "You're really getting a kick out of this, aren't you?"

Avery grinned, narrowly dodging a pedestrian who thought he had the right of way.

"Hey! There are less messy ways to kill yourself!" she howled. "Oh, by the way, I'm thinking of dropping out of school."

"Now why the hell would you do something like that?"

"Um, because it's boring?"

"Just because you're smarter than most of them doesn't mean—"

She put up a hand. "Y'okay. Don't give me the father routine, Tom. And I'm smarter than *all* of them."

I exhaled, smiling inwardly at her never-ending confidence. It was one of the many things I liked about her. "Fine," I said. "But what do your parents think about it?"

"They don't know," she said grinning again.

"This isn't a game, Avery. This is your life. What are you going to do without a college degree?"

She snorted again. Somehow when she did it, it sounded cute.

"You're kidding, right? I could get a job this second at any one of a hundred companies on my radar. Google, Apple—"

This time, I raised my hand. "Alright, alright, I get the picture. But you only have a year left to go. Why not just get it done?"

"I told you. I'm bored. Besides, if the chatter is any indication, we're about to get real busy."

The chatter. She always liked to call it that. The online discussions that spanned the globe, and the topics of which Avery had developed a keen interest in. It was that curiosity that had led to our first introduction.

"Do I have to remind you how dangerous this is?" I said. Jeez. I was really starting to sound old. Even I could hear it in my voice. Next, I'd be telling her to turn down that noise on the radio.

"Danger?" she said. "Danger is my middle name. Ha, ha, ha, ha, ha."

"Have you forgotten...?"

"Of course I haven't forgotten, Tom. I owe you for that. I was stupid. I made a mistake. I don't plan on making the same mistake again."

The mistake she was talking about was a clandestine meeting with one of her chatter contacts. As luck would have it, said contact was not only an illicit money launderer in training, he was also a budding ISIS recruit who happened to live in my building. I'd had a window cracked that night and heard the screams from the rooftop deck. I sprinted up the stairs to find Avery in a chokehold, an angry blade poised just over her left eye. In the commotion that followed, one thing led to another, and said contact found himself airborne. Literally. With a kick to the jewels and a stiff-armed shove, Avery sent him flying off the roof.

She'd played the role of victim well for the cops, but when she returned the next day to thank me, she was all smiles. When I asked her what the smile was all about, she said, "The taste of blood will do that to you, Tom. Don't you know that?"

To this day I don't know whether or not she was joking.

Yes, Avery Van Houten is a special human being, and before you ask, no, I was not, and I am not, attracted to this girl. She's less than half my age. I'm reminded of this fact every time I'm in a car with her.

As this ex-Navy SEAL was now, gripping the door handle as she screeched to a halt a full car's length past the stop sign.

"So, good trip?" she asked.

"Like a Disney ride."

"Any issues with the deceased?" I asked, knowing that she was tracking the chatter. I wasn't going to tell her yet about Agent Baxter. I still didn't know how he fit into the picture.

"None," she said pressing on the gas and flinging us forward.

"Any suspects?"

Avery shook her head. "It was the Bangkok slums. The only reason the police found him was the fire," she said.

"While we're on the subject, did you really think that was necessary?"

I shrugged. "Seemed like a good idea at the time. I got rid of the evidence."

Before you ask, it wasn't at all strange driving through Nashville talking to a young woman in her early twenties about killing another man. It's hard to explain. Young Avery and I had come to a kind of understanding. She had a particular skillset that was perfect for tracking down those I needed to find and, in return, she got to live out her fantasy of being super spy, master hacker and underworld denizen. Besides, she was fun to have around.

It was a stark departure from where she'd come - the Belle Meade family. Father was not only a respected attorney, but a majority shareholder in three of the region's banks. Avery had told me all about her parents. Her father's workaholic tendencies and her mother's alcoholism. While she'd seen much of the world with her parents — one of the perks of being an only child — she had a sparkling rebellious side. If I'm being honest, this made me want to protect her. I could never shake the feeling that she was one online chat away from becoming a CNN story about the dangers of the Internet. So I kept her close. That may seem pretty irresponsible on my part, but I didn't know what else to do.

As I told you before, I take care of my people.

"How's Kyle doing?" Avery asked.

"He's fine. He'll probably be on penicillin for ten weeks after our stop in Bangkok."

"Ew! Gross." She stuck out her tongue. She was still just a kid, and she made me laugh. She straightened up and pulled into a parking lot. She zoomed in under the portico and we jolted to a stop. "Here we are. Say hi to your dad for me."

I gave her a wry smile and opened the door.

"Call me when you're done," she ordered.

"Aye aye, captain," I said as I closed the door. A split second later, she was off, probably to find the nearest Starbucks and her hourly fix of Wi-Fi.

I looked up at the sign. *Sunnyvale Retirement Home*.

I took a deep breath, braced myself, and I walked inside.

THE ADMIRAL

As usual, Rosa was the first to greet me when I stepped inside. She had the beaming smile of a kindly aunt and the patience of a kindergarten teacher. In her profession, she needed it.

"Mr. Tom, it's so good to see you today."

"Hello, Rosa. How's the family?"

She laughed one of those bubbling laughs that made you think that you were the funniest person alive.

"Always growing," she said. "Two more grandbabies coming this month."

"What is that, twelve now?" I asked.

"Very good memory, Mr. Tom." Then her face went slightly more serious. With Rosa, there was no 100% serious. "He is in a mood today, Mr. Tom."

"I'll be careful, I promise."

"You said you were coming, so I had my daughter make you some tamales. Make sure you pick them up on the way out."

"Rosa, you know you didn't need to do that."

Now she reached out and grabbed my hand, put it palm down in hers, then patted the top of it.

"Mr. Tom, for what you did for my son, I can never—"

I cut her off with a broad smile. "Is it the tamales with the chicken or the beef?"

The edge of sadness left her eyes. "Now, Mr. Tom. I know you like the *carne*. The meat I get from a local farm. Grass fed. The best."

She winked at me and patted my hand one last time, and then she was off to her duties. The place ran like a well-oiled machine when Rosa was around. But there was another reason why I considered this woman a godsend.

Other than my mother, she was the only person who could tame the Admiral.

* * *

HIS ROOM WAS DEAD QUIET WHEN I ENTERED. HE WAS THE sole occupant, having chased off a handful of roommates in the preceding years. The bed was made to military perfection. Every picture hanging on the wall looked like it stood at attention. There were the smiling faces of mischievous teens, the black painted faces of frogmen in the jungles of Vietnam. Images of an old Zodiac, half deflated. A rusted submersible. A pile of confiscated foreign weaponry. I'd seen them all a thousand times, so I ignored them like I always did. Instead I focused on the man sitting in front of the window, the sunlight casting its warm glow on his weathered face. I knocked on the door jamb, and he turned slowly towards me.

"Tommy?"

"Hey, Dad."

"It's about time you got here. They've had me waiting for three days."

"Sorry about the delay, I've been busy."

"No harm, no foul," he said. "Now, if you'll get my bag, we can get everything packed up and head on home."

It was the same routine every time. The doctor said it was a part of his condition, but I often wondered if his mind defaulted to decades before, always running out the door at a moment's notice. A bag always packed. Rushed goodbyes in the middle of the night.

"I'll take care of packing in a minute." I said. "Can I get you anything?"

"A cigar and a beer," he said.

"Sure, Dad." It was best to just go along with it. In a moment he would forget, and forget he did.

As his mind wandered and his eyes drifted back to the sunlight, my gaze shifted to the blue flag in the corner, a single star emblazoned in its center. An admiral's flag.

My father was a rare man. He'd enlisted in the Navy at the naïve age of seventeen. Tough as nails, with an attitude to match, he'd quickly been plucked out of the quartermaster's ranks and sent to Coronado to become part of a new breed of warrior. Not only had he endured the rigors of a budding SEAL training program during the Vietnam era, he'd brutally and ruthlessly climbed its ranks.

It should have come to no surprise to the Navy, or to his family, that when it was time to reenlist after his first hitch, he refused to sign on the dotted line. His right hand never raised until the Navy met his demands. Thomas Greer, Sr. had always wanted to be a naval officer. And so, rather than re-enlist, he was commissioned as an Ensign, a SEAL Ensign no less.

His storied career continued through Vietnam and countless minor conflicts you'll never read about in history books. Throughout the 1980s and then up through the first Desert Storm, he became a living legend.

The legend turned back to me.

"Who are you?" he asked.

"I just came to read you a book."

"What book? What do you mean?"

"Any book you want," I said, my tone as dull as a cold sheet.

I'm going to tell you something awful now. The first few times I saw his confusion, his disease slowly wearing away his once razor-sharp mind, I felt a deep sorrow for my father. That had changed. Now, as I looked at him with his expectant, childlike face, I felt only satisfaction. *This is what you deserve, you old prick*.

"So, what will it be today, Admiral? *Treasure Island*, or *Robinson Crusoe?*"

"Have I read those before?" he asked tentatively.

Those two books were some of the only good memories I had of my father. He would return home from whatever mission he'd just completed, wake me up at three in the morning, and pick up wherever he had left off. He'd stop at various points in the stories to tell me how he would've dealt with the pirates or the natives, and how in this day and age, survival on a deserted island could be accomplished with the right preparation. It's no wonder that I went into the profession that I did.

"Why don't you choose?" he said gruffly, his command voice back. I slid the well-worn copy of Robinson Crusoe out of the bookcase and took a seat on the edge of the bed.

"Would you like me to do the voices?"

My father cocked his head in confusion.

"That's what you used to do for me," I blurted.

He cocked his head the other direction, looking frail once again, and every bit his age. "I don't remember."

Once a powerful man who could squeeze out the life of another with his bare hands, my father had shriveled into something unrecognizable. Only two things remained of the

Admiral: his eyes, gray and stern, dry and piercing; and his hair, combed and perfectly parted, now alabaster white.

"The last time we left off we'd just been introduced to Friday," I began. "Now don't laugh at me when I do the voices, I'm not as good as you."

"I can do voices?"

He sounded like a child.

I almost answered, but diving into that well was too painful. So instead I started the story, my mind floating back to my childhood, while my father's drifted to....

I don't know. He just drifted.

STIRRINGS

"How was your visit?" Avery asked when I slipped back into her Hyundai. She didn't give me time to respond, because she saw what I was carrying. "Oh, please tell me those are Rosa's tamales." Not only was Avery gifted in the mental game, she could put away more food than a college linebacker.

"Half of them are yours," I said.

She nodded greedily and then stepped on the gas, whipping my head back into the seat.

"So," she said, "your visit?"

"Good."

"No temper tantrums?"

"No. He was pretty tame."

She navigated the car around a hairpin turn, probably expecting me to chastise her for it. She was quiet, as if she wanted me to say something. Then she said, "I'm sorry you have to see him that way, Tom."

"Yeah, I know."

"I mean, I know you didn't have the best relationship, but—"

"It's okay," I said.

"You know, if you wanted to, you could probably never visit him again — just keep paying the bills. He wouldn't even know it if you didn't show."

"*I* would know, Avery."

Another thing she and I had in common: inattentive fathers. Avery's had groomed her to take over the family business. My father had done the same. And while I hadn't had the courage to strike out on my own, Avery did.

I know it's en vogue to speak badly of younger generations, millennials specifically, but whenever I gazed at Avery, I knew we were all the same.

Think back to when you were a kid. You probably got in trouble or gave your mom and dad grief. Your parents probably didn't like the music you listened to. It is all just history repeating itself. Every generation needs to cling to the shell they've created around themselves. Here I was, looking at talent in plain sight - a capable young woman perfectly suited to her times. Who was I to demand that she be the keeper of the keys for everything I loved when I was a kid?

Avery's father was not oblivious to his daughter's talents, but he was oblivious to the one thing she had that made me want to keep her close, cherish her when her father would not: an emotional thrust — compassion. Something deeper than mere talent, some understanding of the human condition. Maybe that's how she pulled me in and made me unlock my closet of shadows. I sometimes think that today's youth has a better way of expressing and understanding emotion. Maybe that's where the current generational disconnect is. Again, who am I?

"And what about you?" I asked. "Are you gonna tell your parents about dropping out of school?"

"I haven't decided yet."

"What'll you do for money?

It was a stupid question, evidenced by her sideways glance. Avery had two trusts, one set up by her father and another by her maternal grandfather. If she wanted to, she'd never have to work a day in her life. Not only that, she was a modern-day freelancer. From programming to independent investigations, Avery Van Houghton was a new breed of entrepreneur. Lucky for me, her talents lent themselves perfectly to my new profession.

"Anyway," she said with exaggeration, "I checked in with the chatter while you were with your dad. Looks like things are picking up."

"How so?"

"One of your friends is on the move."

"Which friend?"

She smiled. "Number Three."

Good, I thought. "Let's go back to my place. You can brief me there."

"Righto. Oh, and I did some digging on your Agent Baxter."

I'd mentioned his name in passing as I'd gotten out of the car at Sunnyvale. Avery and her steel trap brain. I somehow hid my surprise.

"And?"

She shook her head slowly. "Nada."

"What do you mean?"

"I mean he's a bureau agent, but there's no service record, at least not one that I could find."

"Maybe the FBI is just doing their job and shielding agents from snooping eyes like yours?"

"Maybe." Avery said, not lifting her eyes from the road. "But I've got a bad feeling about him, maybe I should—"

"No." I interjected. "The last thing I need is red flags going up at the Hoover building. Let's let it play out and see what Baxter really wants."

I hadn't told Avery my plan yet, but Agent Baxter's current assignment could help us. I would tell her in due time, but for now it was better to focus on my next target.

BAXTER AND I HAVE A CHAT

A gent Baxter met me at Centennial Park. The public space was dominated by a replica of the Parthenon, a monument I found rather gaudy sitting in the South. We sat down on the steps; me, drenched in sweat from my seven-mile run, and he, decked out like he just stepped off the golf course. He cut a trim figure, more fit than he'd seemed on my plane.

"Nashville sure has grown since the last time I was here," he observed, pulling a thin pad of paper from his pocket.

"I can't say I love the extra traffic, but the inflow of money hasn't hurt," I said, pausing once for a swig from my water bottle.

"How was your stay in San Francisco?" he asked, flipping through his pad, trying to find an empty page.

"Uneventful."

"What do you do when you can't get home right away?"

"Whatever kills the time. Sometimes I see the sights. Sometimes I just walk."

"I thought you flyboys were known for your partying ways."

It was the first glimmer of humor I'd seen from Baxter, although he didn't really smile when he said it.

"Those days are long gone for me," I said.

"Come on," he nudged me, "you don't see a little action on the town? Get to bed at dawn?"

"Listen," I said, "I can't party like I used to. I have a hard enough time keeping off the weight gain."

He stopped what he was doing and looked at me, as if trying to figure out if I was telling the truth. Then, he said matter-of-factly, "You look like you could still be parachuting in on the enemy from ten thousand feet."

Now that made me laugh. "I'm far from where I was."

Time to change the subject.

"So," I said, "what's on the agenda for today?"

Baxter tapped his pen on the pad. "I don't want to get in your way, Tom. I know this assignment seems like a drag, that I'll be riding your hip for months, but I really mean to stay out of your way."

"So you're meeting me during my workout?"

"Oh, well..."

"I'm just kidding. It's not a problem. In fact, I'm actually intrigued by your work."

"You are?"

"Of course I am. Any smart captain would like to know what's being hidden on his ship. Hell, if it'll do some good, I'm all for it."

He looked at me in that way that he did, with a pause like he was waiting for me to say something more. Maybe he was just digesting what I'd just said.

Finally, he spoke. "Well, that's good. I told your superiors that I didn't want to get in the way and I meant it. I mean, I do mean it."

"Fair enough," I said, taking another swig of water. "And I

promise to do the same. Deal?" I stuck out my hand. He looked at it a second, then took it and we shook.

When our hands de-clasped, I stood up to stretch my quads.

"You have to tell me, Ned, was this an assignment you volunteered for or did you get stuck with it?"

He looked uncomfortable for a moment, then he answered. "A little bit of both."

"Let me guess, you pissed somebody off so now, it's payback."

Baxter grinned. "I'm guessing you speak from personal experience?"

"Never piss off the government," I said. "Didn't they teach you that at the academy?"

Baxter chuckled. "I guess I'm a slow learner."

"Yeah, me too."

Something about the fact that Baxter was assigned to me as punishment, but was still taking it seriously, made me feel better about the entire situation. If this was punishment, maybe he wasn't as good as I'd first thought. On the other hand, if he was taking it so well, maybe he was better than I thought.

I tossed the notion away. There'd be time to think on it later.

"Hey, do you mind if we walk while we talk? I didn't get a chance to do a cool-down before you got here."

"Sure," he said.

We walked around the pond, avoiding a crowd of tourists chucking handfuls of bread at a horde of ducks. By the time we'd completed six laps, Agent Baxter had given me a detailed analysis of the smuggling trade. To my surprise, most of it had nothing to do with a plane's cargo hold and everything to do with passengers and, worse, the flight crew.

He described methods of coercion, such as how flight

attendants were blackmailed by drug runners and terrorists alike. Crooks peddled everything from cash to microchips across international borders.

"It's a real problem," he said. "A small problem for now, but one that the Bureau has identified as a tiny leak that could soon burst wide open."

I listened intently and asked questions at regular intervals. He seemed to appreciate my line of questioning because every time I threw one out, he answered animatedly. To his credit, he seemed to have a solid grasp on the subject. By the time we were finished, I almost had the vibe you feel when you walk out of one of those movies where every shadow has the ability to jump out at you. Knowing what Baxter knew could very well make me paranoid, thinking that my own flight team was being coerced. I realized I never really let that thought enter my mind. Sure, we had training for it, but if what Baxter was saying was real, it wouldn't hurt to do a little extra preparation.

"You have flights to Beijing and Tokyo booked for the coming weeks. Is that correct?"

"That's right," I said. "Beijing is all right. It's a million years from where it was the first time I went there, but Tokyo... some of the best food I've ever had."

"Sushi?" Baxter asked.

"Sure, but I'm in it for the noodles. There's this little place I found. A little hole in the wall. You'd never know it was there. A couple of Japanese pilots introduced me to the owner, and now I'm part of the family. *Captain Tommy-san*. I'll take you there when we go."

"Sounds good," Baxter said, "Thanks."

"Hey, us world travelers gotta stick together, right?"

Although we'd established some kind of rapport, Baxter had a certain stiffness to him, like he had worked on trying to loosen up, but the steel in his spine just wouldn't bend.

"Damn, I almost forgot," I said. "Do I need to set anything up for you? I'm sure the airline wouldn't mind if I got you a seat close to the front."

"No, that's fine. It's been taken care of."

"So you got a seat in business class?"

"I prefer sitting in economy," Baxter said.

"Really. A man of the people, are you?"

"I prefer it."

"The leg room and the sleep is a lot better up front."

"I'm good."

"Suit yourself."

I watched him walk away. I liked him. But in truth, you have to know someone to like them, right?

I don't think Ned Baxter was knowable.

But never mind that. With Baxter out of the way for the time being, it was time to get back to business.

My *other* business.

AVERY

It didn't take much to get Avery going. We spent the rest of the day in my condo reviewing the files she'd so meticulously compiled. We went over travel patterns, reviewed CCTV feeds, and finally wrapped up with accomplices.

"So there it is, easy peasy." Avery said. "This one should be a piece of cake."

I studied the target's face one last time and shut the laptop.

"I know I probably should have asked you this before," I said, "but why are you helping me?"

Avery laughed the high-spirited laugh of a girl with her entire life in front of her.

"What other girls my age get to do this? I'm not really the mani-pedi type. This is more fun."

"I'm being serious. And just for your information, this isn't a game."

Avery huffed. "Wow, sorry, *Dad*. I didn't know we were having a talk about my life choices. I'm a big girl, you know."

It was one of those times when her immaturity revealed itself. She could get miffed about the smallest things. It was no wonder her relationship with her parents was on the rocks.

I fixed her with a hard stare. "Avery, I need you to understand what the consequences are if we get caught."

"Sure, sure. We go to jail."

"That's *not* worst case. Worst case is they snatch you up off the street, strap you to a bed, have their way with you, and then torture you to death. Maybe a combination of the last two."

Her eyes dropped and the corners of her mouth straightened, as immature apathy gave way to primal fear.

"It's not likely," I continued, "but it's possible. Jail is also a very real possibility, especially with an FBI agent snooping around."

"But I thought you said he was just a paper pusher."

"We don't know the truth, until we know the truth," I said, repeating a line my father had drilled into me as a teenager. "Besides, a paper-pushing FBI agent is still an FBI agent."

"So where are you going with this, Tom? We've covered jail and death. What about the upside? What's the best-case scenario?"

I frowned. She still wasn't getting it.

"Best case is we get away scot free, the local cops in some backwater slum don't catch us, the FBI leaves us alone. But then years from now, the dreams will keep coming. At first they're just dreams, memories of what we've done. And then they turn into nightmares. I know my conscience is clean, but you? You've never been through this. I need to know that you understand."

"Tom, I somehow get the impression that you believe all the stereotypes about my generation. That our brains have been desensitized to violence through video games and movies and our shit music."

"It's not that," I said.

"I've read the studies, Tom. I know what traumatic events can do to a person." She reached out and laid a friendly hand on top of mine. "That's why I'm doing this. Sure, it's fun and there'll be some secret glory about it all in the end. But you helped me out of a tough spot. More importantly, you opened up to me, and I want to help."

We sat there for a long minute.

When you're being inundated by the crashing waves of pain, it's hard to see a lifeline. Avery had been mine. She had caught me at a bad moment, arriving late one night after a marathon session at the library. Her backpack had been full of books, and mine had been full of booze.

It wasn't my proudest moment, but I guess in moments of weakness, helping hands are most welcome.

I pulled my hand out from under hers and gave her a pretend punch in the shoulder. "I just want to make sure that you know we're nearing the point of no return. You're still a kid, a great kid who has so much to offer the world."

"What? And your life is over, old man?" she said with a smile.

"No, I didn't say that. But this is like round six or seven for me. This is just round one for you."

"Boxing metaphors? Really, Tom? I thought you were smarter than that."

I couldn't hold back the chuckle. "Look, Avery, you've done so much for me already. If you want to walk away now—"

"I'm not walking away, Tom. We're in this together."

What can I say? I tried. Despite her immaturity, she was an adult. She had gotten the warning, and I know she processed the dangers, although those dangers were probably sprinkled with a fair amount of glitter in her mind. It was one thing to know about the dark things that went bump in the night. It was another to face them head-on in a rubbish-strewn ditch.

"One last thing," I said. "The job in Bangkok was easy. And if I've learned anything in my advanced age, it's that when things seem the easiest, that's exactly when you need to be ready for a counterattack. You're going to be my eyes and ears. We need to be careful. You need to be careful."

"Point taken," she said. "Now, can we go downstairs and get some pizza? I'm starved."

We were about to leave when my cell phone buzzed. I looked at the number, which activated an electrified pit of anxiety in my stomach.

The voice on the other end said, "*It's happened again.*"

I hung up the phone and turned to Avery and repeated what the caller had said.

"I'm coming with you," she said.

"No."

She looked at me. "Yes."

"I don't want this for you."

She gathered up her things. "I don't care."

THE ADMIRAL

W e pulled up to the end of a long, gravel drive.
"Are you sure?" Avery asked me.
"I don't see why not."

She pulled forward and her tires crunched as we made our way down the path. How many times had I been down this winding boulevard?

The house soon came into view, but we didn't take a right. Instead, when we hit the fork, we took the left and dipped down, splashing through a shallow stream, tree branches scraping the roof of the car. The road was no longer well-tended, and a deep rut had been sliced right down the middle by the rains. For the first time, Avery took her time. At one point, I had to get out and guide her around a tree that had fallen in a recent storm.

We made it safely up and down the hillocks, fields left unattended on each side. I saw the river in the distance, engorged and chocolate brown.

I barely registered any of it. I was too focused on the road ahead.

Finally, we broke back out into the sunlight. The long grass had almost overtaken the road.

"Let's walk the rest of the way," I suggested. "I don't want your car to get stuck."

Avery nodded, put the car in park and turned off the engine.

I stepped out into the humid air, pushing through the grass that reached up to my chest. I could have walked the rest of the way blindfolded. We went up a small hill and then a sharp left at the split maple that had been struck in a lightning storm years ago. I touched the maple and moved on, getting my first glimpse of the rusted wrought iron up ahead.

When we made it to the fence, I stopped. There he was, lying on the ground, surrounded by headstones. Same as the other times. How my father made his way a good ten miles to his childhood home, I never knew. Maybe there was some of his wiliness still left. He'd somehow snuck out of the nursing home in a robe, completely barefoot.

"Do you think he's okay?" Avery asked. Still standing at the gate, I did a once-over of my father. His legs had tiny slashes all over where branches, thorns, and razor-sharp grass had sliced him. His calloused feet were caked in dirt, but otherwise sound, as far as I could see.

I'm not sure how long I stood there staring at him. I can't really tell you what I was thinking. I didn't feel pity, nor anger. He was a grown man, even if he'd lost most of his mental faculties. To come all this way, he obviously still had some of his marbles left. Part of me was honestly fascinated that he had come all this way; there was something amazing about the human mind. Some small part of my father's brain had cocooned itself, perfectly preserved, and guided him, at various intervals, back to the family cemetery. His lucidity kicked in just enough to allow him to convince people who didn't know him that he was sane.

"Tom?" Avery's voice cut through my thoughts. When I analyzed it, it sounded as if it were the third or fourth time she was calling it.

"Sorry, just daydreaming."

"It's okay. Do you want me to get him?"

I took a deep breath. "You don't mind?"

"He's nicer to me than he is to you."

She was right about that. The Admiral could be a mean old cuss, but he was never a mean old cuss to a pretty young girl. I gave Avery a nod and she eased the iron gate open. It creaked loudly. The sound did not disturb my father's slumber.

That wonderful young woman who held more compassion in a single eyelash than most people I've met have in their entire body, walked up to my father slowly and bent down. She laid a hand on his knee, pressing it gently. He stirred and, then, one of his hands reached out to grab a headstone. He whined like a newborn. There were no tears. There were rarely tears, but his face twisted in anguish. When his eyes creaked open, he moaned in a way that marked unbearable human sadness. I had to walk away as the sound turned into a low wail. Avery's voice was soothing now. Over and over she said, "It's okay."

As my chest constricted and the sounds of my father's grief died down, I couldn't help but think that this young woman, this kind soul, was taking care of both of us. Two SEALs, tough as nails, reduced to caregiving from a girl in her early twenties.

"Tom, I need your help," Avery said. I didn't want to go back, but I did. I gripped the top of the iron gate with a steel grasp, my right foot hovering. It wanted to avoid the earth within the cemetery like it was a river of lava. But I stepped in, anyway. My gaze avoided the headstones and, instead, focused keenly on my father who had coiled into a tight ball, arms wrapped around his knees.

True concern etched Avery's features when I glanced at her, equally for my dad and for myself. I'd gone into a bit of a tailspin the last time this had happened. In fact, it had led to my escapades in Bangkok.

I kneeled down and brushed a rare stray hair from my father's forehead.

"It's okay, Dad. I'm gonna help you up now." He relaxed at the sound of my voice, and his arms unclenched from his legs. "Okay. Slow and easy now."

I hooked my hands under his armpits and heaved him up tenderly. It almost broke my heart to feel how fragile he was. I could have hoisted him over one shoulder if I wanted. He weighed no more than a half-full bag of flour. This was a man who, when I was a teenager, would stand in front of me with his shirt off, and tell me to punch him over and over again in his stomach. Even when I was an all-state tight end, we had our duels. His rock-solid abs against my angst-filled youth.

"Tommy?" he asked, looking into my eyes. His wavered as if he couldn't focus on my face.

"Yeah, it's me, Dad. Come on, we're gonna take you home."

"Home," he mouthed, without saying a word.

"Here, I can help," Avery said. She slipped under his other arm, even though it was unnecessary. It would have been easy for me to cradle him in my arms, but maybe this was more fitting. Two friends carrying the remains of a once-great man walked out of the cemetery together.

I closed the gate behind us. My father looked back one final time, a wistful look, a look of regret and pain. Then, his head swiveled back, the maudlin glaze returning.

I nodded to Avery, who had stepped back onto the path, the long grass swishing as we stepped.

"Ain't this a metaphor for life," she said between pants.

All I could think was that this was the last time. I could no longer be part of the decline of the Admiral. And I could never again visit this cursed place.

I needed redemption.

I needed the salve for my battered soul.

I needed to kill.

THE AFTERMATH

"I need to get out of town," I said.

We sat outside my father's retirement home, digesting all that had happened. Dad had been all but comatose on the drive back, but as the blocks got shorter and we pulled up to the front door, he went into a fit of hysterics. It had taken a team of orderlies, a syringe full of sedatives, and four-point restraints to finally get him to calm down.

It was the restraints that had done it for me. Something about those bony hands desperately clutching at nothing. I couldn't watch anymore. But Avery stayed as I'd paced in the parking lot, too much of a coward to watch what my father had become.

"He's going to be okay, you know," Avery said. "I bet he won't even remember."

I laughed at the irony. No doctor could tell us what my father could and couldn't remember. Ninety-five percent of the time he didn't know who I was; and yet, somehow, he'd trekked all the way to our family grave site.

His mind was in tatters, but what was etched forever on those tatters, only my father could tell you.

"How do you think he did it?" said Avery. "It's amazing, really. Maybe we should talk to the doctors about it. See if there's a chance—"

"Let's get out of here," I said. "You can drop me back at the park and I can run home."

Avery hesitated. She wanted to talk, find a solution, some sliver of hope.

I wanted to leave.

"Why don't I just take you home, Tom?"

"No." I snapped, quickly recovering. "I'm sorry. I don't mean to take it out on you, it's just that... "

"I know," she said. But did she really?

TRUTH TO POWER

Truth to power.

What does that mean?

Does it mean that whomever holds the truth holds the power? Or vice-versa?

These were my thoughts as we executed another flawless landing in San Francisco. What I really needed was a nice long walk. That's one of the only things I don't like about being stuck in a plane for hours. The lack of fresh air. The inability to really stretch my legs.

"Welcome to San Francisco, ladies and gentlemen," I announced over the intercom. "The local time is ten forty-three in the morning." I continued my spiel, sticking to my usual script. I was never one of those funny-ha-ha pilots. Kyle played that part when I gave him the mic on rare occasions. He was a brilliant pilot, but his couth left something to be desired.

Agent Baxter was our last passenger on board as I made my way through the otherwise empty aircraft. He sat there clicking away on a laptop, and looked up as I approached.

"Didn't anyone tell you that all work and no play makes Ned a dull boy?" I asked.

I'd taken to him during our limited time together. Sure, he was a damper on my plans, but he had wit. I was actually somewhat looking forward to learning from him in the coming months.

Oh right. You're probably wondering why.

Well, I've never been a complainer.

I take that back. I can't say never. I'm a stickler on such generalities. I guess we were all complainers at some point, namely when we were children. It's like the use of the word 'literally'. It's an absolute word, and yet, so many people use it incorrectly, and as frequently as the words 'and' or 'but'.

The crowd literally exploded when Elvis entered the building.

There I go again. I'm boring you. You don't need to know this stuff. You want to hear about Agent Baxter and how he was going to screw up my plans.

He wasn't. Not exactly.

Before I went off on that last tangent, I was going to say that I had an epiphany. You know the old saying, "If life gives you lemons... blah, blah, blah." Well, I've had to learn to fully embrace that statement, albeit with some modification. What I learned was this: You don't have to make them into lemonade. You can save time by just learning to like the taste of lemons, period. The last five years have been one train wreck after another. If I'd fallen down on my knees every time I got hurt, I'd need bilateral knee replacements by now.

My point is that I had to look at the unexpected addition of Agent Baxter to my life in a positive light. Sure, having an FBI agent as your tagalong does make for a heaping spoonful of crumbs in your butter, but maybe not entirely so.

Baxter's job was to dissect a budding smuggling empire. By helping him, I could learn. I've always been pretty quick on the uptake. You show me something once, and it just sticks.

Take the first time I took control of an aircraft. I'd watched my instructor for an hour, and then when it was my turn, it just fit. He later accused me of lying on my application. I promptly fired him and hired a female pilot who believed me when I said I'd never flown before. She called me a natural after just one hop in the air.

Damn. I'm rambling again. Sorry you had to see that. I'm not used to spilling my innermost thoughts to anyone. Now that the floodgates are open, I'll try to spare you the fluff and get right to the fodder.

Back to Baxter.

The guy had really done his homework. I'm not sure why it surprised me that someone would care enough about a job to do 150% more than the next man. Baxter had timelines, airline manifests, basically anything I would've suggested to get started, including pickup and drop-off locations. When he asked if I thought he'd missed anything, I told him honestly that I couldn't think of a thing that he'd missed.

Well, there was one thing: *Me*.

Agent Baxter clapped his laptop shut and packed the rest of his belongings into a single carry-on bag. Efficient.

"Where are you staying?" I asked him.

"Don't know yet. I didn't get a chance to find a place."

"If you need a recommendation, you've got my number."

"Thanks, Tom." He'd finally gotten into the habit of calling me by my first name. *Bravo on the personality points, Neddy*.

"No problem," I said. "Hey, I'm not sure if you're headed straight to work, but I never stop in San Fran without getting a sourdough bowl of chowder while I'm here. You wanna join me?"

In for a penny...

"I don't want to impose."

"My treat."

He hesitated. Honestly, I thought he would've jumped at the chance to pick my brain some more. I'd taken him for a workaholic.

"You know what? I actually have plans. Rain check?"

"Sure," I said, surprisingly let down. "I fly home to Nashville tomorrow. When did you say you'd be coming?"

"The day after tomorrow," he said, following me out of the aircraft and onto the jet bridge.

"Give me a call when you get into town. We can have dinner at one of my favorite restaurants."

"What's it called? I'll take a look at the menu beforehand."

Of course you will, I thought.

"Cork and Cow. It's in downtown Franklin. Steaks galore, and the shrimp and scallop gnocchi is a bowl of heaven."

"Sounds like a plan," he said. "Now, if you don't mind, I'll be on my way."

He didn't offer a hand to shake or a formal goodbye. He just left.

I watched him go and noticed that he never took his eyes off of his destination. That man was focused. His mind always on *The Next Thing*. Like I said before, he was a real bloodhound.

Careful, Tom. You've got work to do.

THE SPECTER OF DEATH

It was Nietzsche who said, and I quote, "All truly great thoughts are conceived while walking."

I know what you're thinking. "A quote? Really, Tom? I didn't think you were that kind of guy."

Sorry, folks, but I am. As corny as it sounds, I'm a sucker for quotes. From George Washington to Helen Keller, I read them all. I write them on tiny index cards and file them away for later. Quotes are like little snippets of history. If we're smart, we jot them down and put them in our pocket for a crappy day.

Back to my walk.

You might think that after a stay overseas, a flight crew would reacquaint itself with The Motherland by hanging in a few bars, or blowing a month's salary in a high-end San Francisco hotel. Maybe the young ones. Maybe the ones who haven't learned yet. Hell, maybe Kyle was out shagging his way through the barely legal tech populace.

But not me. Whenever I came to San Francisco, I wanted to walk. For miles and miles, up and down the hills. It was my personal challenge. But not just a challenge. It gave me time to think. Time to talk to myself.

No, not in a crazy schizophrenic way of talking to myself. In a therapeutic, let's get back to my Zen kind of way of talking to myself.

Over the previous five years, I'd logged hundreds, if not thousands of miles, not only in San Francisco but in various major hubs in the US. I'd worn a virtual path down certain streets, seemingly on a meandering course, but my body always knew which way to go. My mind fully engaged in that day's thoughts. After I landed in San Francisco, and made sure my team knew of our next departure, I checked into my hotel, threw my things on the bed, and went for a stroll.

A casual lunch with a casual beer led to more miles, through parks, past countless restaurants, under the shadows of buildings that looked like the next great earthquake would finally knock them to their senses.

And on I went. I replayed the scene with the fire and my complete lack of emotion after taking a man's life. You probably want to know who that person was and why I decided to kill him. It doesn't matter. At least, not yet. It's not germane to this part of the story.

What was important, as I followed a streetcar back down towards the cool coastline, was that my euphoria was waning. My ecstatic exuberance for life that the flames had wrought was failing me.

That's where these walks came in handy.

"Get your body moving, Tom."

"More thinking, less feeling, Tom."

Always more thinking. That's where I found the answers.

But not today, at least not until I found my favorite Italian dive, the garlic oozing invisibly from its centuries-old façade. Mario, the proprietor, greeted me by name and escorted me to my usual table. You'd think that I'd been there a thousand times and was a regular every afternoon. But I wasn't.

Maybe once a month. I think it was the *Godfather*-esque décor that had first pulled me in, but today it was the familiar smells, the delicious combination of olive oil and roasted tomatoes, garlic and seafood.

I tried to relax through Mario's jabbering as he cleared a table with one hand and kept another on my shoulder. He asked me questions and I somehow replied, my thoughts still mulling over my latest mental lapse. I thought, "A salad would be appropriate." I had a lot more walking to do. But when a crusty loaf of bread came out, I devoured it. No salad for me.

Dinner was a delicate linguine with clam sauce, the lemon so fresh that I could smell the orchard it was grown in. I barely came up for air, and then I was finished.

All the while, I measured my invisible joviality meter as it dipped well below halfway. Stupid name for a stupid emotion, but it works for me.

Sorry, Tom. Euphoria gone.

I politely declined dessert, even as Mario offered to give it to me on the house. I thanked him for his kindness, probably said something about how wonderful his establishment was, what a treat it was that I could visit him on every one of my stays in San Francisco.

I don't really know what I said. It was like the feeling you get when you've been driving and talking on the phone. You get done with the conversation and you realize you've gone thirty miles and you don't remember a thing. Spooky. You somehow dodged cars, sped up and slowed down, and you don't remember a bit of it. Scary, right?

And so I left Mario and his evening clientele. A mix of hipsters, high-end professionals, and locals who threw dagger-filled looks at their respective interlopers.

Back to my walking. On I went, calculations already done in my head. All I had to do was set my feet to moving. Dark was coming now, and for some reason I veered off my normal path. I usually liked to stay in the light, on the fringes of the more touristy areas. But inexplicably, indecipherably, I was pulled another way.

I won't tell you that the darkness and dank that I soon found was a mirror to my soul. I'm not that poetic. I think what I was really looking for was a fight.

Subconsciously, I wanted someone to jump me from the shadows. I needed to feel the basest human violence. Maybe that would bring it back. Maybe then, happiness would return. Maybe that's all that I needed.

So I called to them silently. *Come to me, demons of the night. Tom Greer is waiting.* Despite my inner turmoil, I strolled with a casual gait. I passed a trio of homeless men pissing on a wall, all three giggling to themselves. Not a one looked up at my passing.

And then I saw it out of the corner of my eye. A flicker of movement inside a car fifty feet away. It took a full block before the headlights flicked on and moments later, it was following me.

Good, I thought, *let's make things interesting.*

So, deeper I went. Past piles of garbage that may or may not have been the makeshift homes of one or more of the countless San Francisco vagabonds. My senses came alive. I tracked the creeping vehicle, even as I swept the area ahead of me for lurking danger, my posture never wavered. My hands tucked comfortably in my pockets.

See? No threat, people. Come and get me.

Inside, I was getting antsy now. As the hours had passed, I have to admit something. The specter of death had returned. Like a vulture to carrion. It smelled my unease. I needed to do something about it.

I was so absorbed in thirty different thoughts that I misread the cues. No, not something ethereal. Not some message sent down from the heavens or up from hell, but a simple, everyday mistake.

I turned down the wrong street. I literally didn't read the sign that said 'Dead End'. Fitting, don't you think?

So when I came to the end of the alleyway and found it impassable, I stopped like a man who'd just been punched in the face.

Great, I thought.

And then I turned slowly, knowing exactly what I would find. The car that had been following me closed in. The headlights flickered, and up came the high beams. I put a hand up to shield my eyes. I took a deep breath and waited.

CONFRONTATION

I expected a hand to reach out of the car window holding a pistol or one of those tacky Uzis. I was ready for it. Well, as ready as an unarmed man can be ready. But, mathematically, I had decent odds. Shooting a diving target over forty feet away is a difficult thing to do, especially when you were shooting one-handed.

I thought that option unlikely.

The next option I expected was to hear the revving engine. The confined space would make it easy to crush me against the wall behind my back. I could pull off the cheesy Hollywood jump, run and roll over the car. I've done it before, but that took perfect timing.

To my surprise, the gun and the battering ram never materialized. Instead, I heard the door open, and then it shut.

A male voice asked, "Are you lost?" I still couldn't see him.

For some reason, I didn't answer. I think I was goading the person, egging him on. *Come on you bastard. Fight me. Fight me, so I can put my hands on you.*

"I said, are you lost?" The voice had authority now.

This time, I answered. "Just took a wrong turn," I said.

The man stepped out of the glare. I could see his outline now. "Maybe you should head back. We've had two muggings in as many nights in this part of town. I can give you a ride..." the voice screeched to a halt like a horse planting its front hooves and throwing its rider.

Here it comes, I thought. The charade was being cast aside. Inside my pockets, my fists were balled. *Come on.*

"Hey, aren't you that guy?" the man asked, stepping closer. He was on the smaller side. 5'8" to my 6'4", medium build. I still couldn't see his face. "You are that guy, aren't you?" Still, I didn't answer. "Hey, are you drunk? High?"

"I am not drunk or high," I said through my teeth. The coming violence tasted like steel on my tongue. The man just stood there, appraised me for what seemed like an eternity. *Do something*, I urged silently. *Make a move.*

But he didn't.

Why wasn't he doing something? Anything? Couldn't he see that I was in no position to launch the first salvo?

"You *are* that guy," the man said. I saw his hand reach into his pocket.

Here it comes, I thought. *Brace yourself.*

I was ready to dive, but before I did, I saw the illuminated screen of a cellphone, now unsheathed from his pocket. The stranger tapped on the screen, his face cast with the phone glow. It was chubby and did not match his general physique. An alcoholic maybe, or maybe it was just genetic. I instantly tagged him as Bubble Face. Don't ask me why.

Bubble Face nodded, still looking at the screen. "I knew it, it is you!"

The violence inside of me threatened to build to a crescendo, a blood red volcano begging to erupt.

"What are you talking about?" I heard myself say slowly.

The man held up the screen and tapped it. I watched a familiar scene, an unruly passenger singing to his audience, camera panning all the way around the first-class cabin. Concerned looks from the crew. And then there was my face. The back and forth conversation, and then finally the altercation.

"Oh man, I love that part," Bubble Face said. "You really got him good. How long did it take him to come to?"

"Not long," I grumbled.

For the first time, the man must have caught my unease, because he said, "Hey, I didn't mean to interrupt you. I just saw you walking and you looked familiar. You know this video has a quarter of a million views already? You're famous, man."

Famous? That was the last thing I needed. I hadn't seen anyone recording the episode, but that's the new world, isn't it? You never know who could be filming. When did we lose all privacy?

I couldn't figure out what he was waiting for. A detailed explanation of how I'd subdued the unruly passenger? Or maybe he wanted an autograph. Maybe that's what it was. *Sorry pal, no autographs today.*

"Hey, I was serious about what I said before," the man said. "It's not safe around here after dark."

"What are you, neighborhood watch?" I asked. I tried to sound funny, but I heard the edge in my tone.

The man bristled and when he said his next words, I swear he grew to an inch over six feet. "No, I'm a cop."

Good job, Tom. Piss off a cop days after you killed a man.

In this game, it ain't straight three strikes and you're out. You only get one.

Damage control time.

"I'm sorry, officer. I didn't see any markings on your car, and you're not..."

"Dressed for the occasion?" the cop said, smiling.

"Right, well either way, I'm sorry. I've just got a lot on my mind. I think I got sidetracked a few streets back."

"I get it. I've been in my fair share of scraps," the officer said. "It's not easy to let go. The adrenaline does a funny thing, doesn't it?"

I just nodded. *Go along with it, Tom. Just go along.*

Little did the cop know, it had nothing to do with adrenaline. It had everything to do with the fact that I'd wanted him to be someone he wasn't. A petty thug, or a drug overlord. Someone dangerous and odious who deserved my wrath.

"So, do you think you'll get in trouble?" he asked.

"I'm sorry, what do you mean?"

"You know, for hitting that guy. You can't really see it on the video, but I know you hit him, it's the only way that he went down like that."

To be honest, I hadn't really thought about it. I'd given a short statement at the airport after landing, but I had yet to receive a phone call from headquarters. I groaned inwardly at the thought.

"No, I think I'll be okay," I said.

"Well, if they give you any grief about it, you tell them to check out YouTube. This time tomorrow, half of America's going to hailing be you as a hero."

"He was just a drunk," I said. "Happens all the time."

The cop chuckled. "Hell, *I* know that and *you* know that, but America doesn't know that. To your average Joe, physical violence is only something they see on television or in the movies. This," he said, tapping his phone, "this is the stuff that people want to see. An idiot hitting a woman, and then an airline captain who, no offense, looks like the guy who should be on the airlines' commercials, jumps in and just takes this guy out." He whistled through his teeth. "But you know what? I'm almost sad to see that America's going to miss what was truly impressive." He turns the phone so I can see the screen, and then he drags the scroll. He gets the video to the exact point that he wants to replay. The video resumes.

"This, this is what's impressive to me. This is what's going to be impressive to the rest of us who have dealt with this crap before." He paused the video. It was a close up of my face. "Look at that, man. Ice cold, that face. No nerves. Like a walk on the beach before dinner time. I'm calling it now, by the time you wake up tomorrow morning, you're going to have some nickname online like Cool Hand Luke, or Vanilla Ice."

"I doubt that," I said.

"Doubt it all you want, Captain, but you're a celebrity now." The cop stuffed the phone back into his pocket. "I've gotta head back to the precinct, can I give you a lift? At least let me get you out of this neighborhood."

"I think I'll be okay."

He tried one more time. I let him down politely.

"Have it your way, just watch out for the meth heads, they like to get rowdy at about one A.M."

"Thanks, I'll keep that in mind," I said. Minutes before, I would have made a beeline for those drug addicts, but now the anger was gone, replaced by confusion and exhaustion.

"Well, have a nice night, Captain. My buddies aren't going to believe I met you." He paused, and this time I thought he really was going to ask me for an autograph, or even worse, take a selfie with me, but he didn't. Maybe he thought better of it. With a wave, he was back in his car, high beams shifting to normal, and then he backed out the way he'd come. But then he pulled forward again and poked his head out of the window.

"Hey, Captain? One suggestion."

"What's that?"

"Next time you decide to roam the humble streets of San Francisco, try not to be so conspicuous."

I had no idea what he meant until he pulled away and I looked down. *You're the idiot, Tom.*

I hadn't realized I'd been wearing my uniform the entire day. That's one way to put a target on your back.

DEEP THOUGHTS WITH TOM GREER

You may or may not have picked up on this, but I'm a details kind of guy.

Here's an example from work: Not only do I take personal responsibility for the flying, navigating, and general running of my aircraft, I want to know if we're low on Sprite, heavy on pretzels, or if there's a woman in 38A who's well into her third trimester.

Sure, I go a little overboard about what I need to know. But what do they say about prior preparation?

Never mind. It's not important. Suffice it to say that a teeny detail, like wearing my uniform out in public, is a glaring example that something had gone wrong.

You're probably reading this and going back to your "Tom is cuckoo" hypothesis. I'm not going to lie. For a few minutes, it felt that way, but I'm not one to dwell on my shortcomings. Few though they may be.

Pick yourself up, Tom. Dust yourself off. Move on. Learn from your mistakes.

Those were my father's words. Get a scraped knee? Shake

it off, and get back on that bike. Break your arm in three places? Grin and bear it.

There you go. I see it again. Your mind's going off on a rabbit trail. Tom's got daddy issues. I respond to you by saying, "Who doesn't have daddy issues?" I could sit here and complain about how my dad didn't love me enough, or he never came to my soccer games, but I'm done being bitter.

Whatever I went through with my father, it molded me into the man that I am today, and the man that I was that night in San Francisco, marveling at the fact that I had worn my uniform for hours after my shift had ended.

That explained the stares, I thought in that stinking alleyway.

So, I did what I always did, and hopefully I'll keep doing it until the day I die. I shrugged it off. It was a stupid mistake. I laughed at myself, and I put one foot in front of the other.

Oh, are you still there? Are you waiting for some words of wisdom? Some pontification that will make you feel better about what you've read here? Well, try this one on for size: *Don't pity yourself, and don't pity me. Pity the poor fool lying in the gutter who doesn't know any better*.

See, I told you I was bad at this. That's why I love quotes. Next time, I'll stick to that.

For now though, let's get back to the kill. If you'll notice above, the fasten seat belt sign is lit.

Turbulence ahead.

TARGET NUMBER TWO

The next morning, I was up at 4:00am pounding out push-ups and pull-ups until it felt like my arms would fall off. My scheduled Uber ride arrived at quarter to five. Perfect. The right way to start off the morning.

The driver wasn't the Chatty Cathy sort, which was fine with me. When I got to the airport, I breezed through security. By the time I made it to the gate, I had regained some measure of my sanity. I was even cordial when Agent Baxter walked up five minutes later.

"Good morning, Captain."

"Coffee or tea" I asked, pointing to his Starbucks mug.

"Tea."

"Do they give you a hard time for that in the Bureau?"

Baxter shrugged like it didn't matter. "I was wondering if I could run some things by you? I figured we could start a sort of routine now. That way as we go, I won't have to steal as much of your time."

I patted him on the back and ushered him onto the plane.

"I'm all yours until we get to Seattle, but then it's time for the cockpit."

Baxter peppered me with questions as we sat next to each other on the flight. They were the basic things like boarding procedures, cursory inspections, and crew manifests. Then there were the more interesting deep dives, like, "What is the typical ratio of males to females on a flight?" "How often do airport staff inspect cargo holds?" And the one that got my attention, "If you had to kill someone on a plane, how would you do it?"

I answered that one with a laugh, "I wouldn't."

Baxter nodded, did not laugh, and jotted down some notes. I tried to see what he was writing but it was in some kind of shorthand and I couldn't pick up much more than a few numbers and letters.

If there was one thing I learned about Baxter on that flight, it was that his mind never forgot a detail. He would reference one of the answers I'd given two hours earlier, repeating my words almost verbatim. The guy knew his stuff.

It was surreal though. The entire time I scanned him for any recognition that *I* was a suspect. He was either an elite poker player or completely consumed with his job. I picked the latter, considering his earnestness and the stack of notepads he had in his bag. It was surprising that he never once pulled out an electronic gadget. I expected a laptop or even a phone for taking notes.

I asked him about it at some point and he said, "I only use computers for reports. Details stick when I write them by hand."

* * *

WE SPLIT UP IN SEATTLE SO THAT I COULD GET READY FOR my flight. Baxter said he had to report in with his superiors.

I checked my messages after ironing out the details of the

flight to Tokyo. Nothing from the retirement home, but there was a quick text from Avery.

"Have a nice flight," it said. That was code for *check your messages.*

When you're on an endeavor such as mine, secrecy is paramount. Avery couldn't just text me a target's dossier. It was encrypted on my phone, but we'd gone over it, and I had a firm grasp of who the man was. Avery was tracking him that very moment.

It was Avery who'd come up with the ingenious solution of how to get me information. It wasn't anything as mundane as an email left in a draft folder or a sinister sounding visit to the dark web. She'd developed a game, an application to be sold on iTunes and Google Play. She told me it sold three copies every month and had an average 2.5 star rating. It was a knock-off of the popular Candy Crush game, but it wasn't the game that was important. It was what was embedded inside that was vital to my success.

Instead of video ads that would play when you clicked through, Avery had developed a messaging system that played like an innocuous ad. It was all in cartoon form so that if someone was watching over my shoulder, or if the message somehow got into the wrong hands, they wouldn't know how to decipher it. But sitting in a private lounge of the Seattle Airport with my headphones on, I watched the fake ad and smiled. Avery had a firm grasp of this one and already my senses were tingling for the kill.

* * *

THE FLIGHT FROM SEATTLE TO TOKYO WAS BUSIER THAN I would have liked. Five passengers got sick. It had nothing to do with my flying and everything to do with the fact that all five passengers, an entire family from Tampa, had eaten bad ceviche in the airport.

Don't ever eat ceviche in an airport.

It was a miserable experience for any human being, being trapped in a metal tube while your body rebelled out of both ends. My team was on it, and you'd be surprised at how helpful other passengers can be when they see their peers in distress. We were also lucky enough to have a group of CRNAs who were on their way to China on a volunteer mission. The anesthetists had cases of IV fluid in their special carry-on baggage that came in handy. Once we'd set up a sort of triage space in the back of the plane, close to the bathroom, everyone could breathe easier. Well, except for those passengers who were too close to the tail of the plane.

I checked in with Agent Baxter a couple times, but each time he said if he had anything new it could wait until we got to Japan. I marveled at the fact that he was sandwiched between a severely overweight man and a fidgety seven-year-old, but there wasn't a scrap of discomfort on Baxter's face. In fact, he looked content, like he'd just walked out of the best massage of his life. I secretly wished we could bottle that attitude and give it to all of our passengers.

* * *

IT WASN'T UNTIL WE WERE AN HOUR AND A HALF OUTSIDE of Tokyo that I saw my target and looked into his eyes. He had no idea who I was other than the captain of the plane. I started from the front of the first-class cabin, checking on my passengers and giving out miniature airplanes to the children. The kids always liked to say hi to the captain.

The man I was looking for was in row seven. He had noise-canceling headphones on and his eyes were closed, his head bobbing to the music.

I tapped him on the shoulder. The eyes flew open in surprise. He was all skinny jeans and skinny shirt, black on black on black. He even had a thin streak of eyeliner over each eye. Annoyance flashed in his eyes for a moment, then he saw who I was. He removed the closest side of his headphones and said, "Yes?"

"I wanted to see if you needed anything?"

He looked me up and down again and then stared at my name badge.

"I didn't know captains served champagne." He grinned. I saw the glint of gold on his lower left canine, just where Avery said it was.

"I'm not serving champagne, but I can get you some if you'd like," I said, all smiles.

"Yeah, I'm good, but thanks."

"Are you going to Tokyo for business?"

"What are you, the FBI?"

"No, they're down in economy class," I said.

"Are you serious?" he asked.

"About the FBI? Yes."

"No, about wanting my life story."

"I'm just curious." I said, still smiling.

I was taking a risk. Avery wouldn't like it. But something about seeing this worthless piece of trash sitting right below me triggered hot flashes of wild emotion inside me.

"Yeah, I'm going there for business," he said in a huff.

"What do you do?"

"I'm a DJ, okay, can I—?"

I sat down on the arm rest, so he had to scoot over to make room. He looked at me like I was crazy.

"I knew you were someone important. I meet a lot of important people from all walks of life on this job. I love to get to know them. As far as an education is concerned, it beats the second floor of the public library. So, a DJ, huh? You mean like with a turntable and records and all that? You do that scratching stuff?"

He snorted. "No, man. I mean, I used to. But everything's digital now." He pulled a small memory stick out of his pocket. "My entire life's work is right here."

"No kidding." I said, marveling at it like it was an alien artifact.

He let it drop back into his pocket.

"Alrighty then," I said, standing up. "If we can do anything for you, make the trip more comfortable, please let us know, Mister— ?"

He sat there with an incredulous look, like he couldn't believe I was asking for his name. "I thought you said you knew me."

"I said I knew you were someone important."

"Matsuyama," he finally offered.

Target acquired, I thought in my head.

"Matsuyama," I said, as if trying it on for the first time. "It's a pleasure to meet you, Mr. Matsuyama. Now, I should probably get back to flying the plane. I don't like my co-pilot taking all the credit for perfect landings."

I gave him a wink.

He made that annoyed look that kids give parents when told they're supposed to eat their vegetables. His wave was more of a wave off.

I locked eyes with him one last time. Those deep green eyes, the eyes of a cunning snake, a pied piper.

I'll see you again soon, Edgar Matsuyama.

EDGAR

Tokyo always brought back a flood of memories. Dad had done two tours in Japan, and I'd fallen in love with the culture. Believe it or not, Japanese was my first language. That happens when you move to a country at seven months of age.

There were plenty of sights and sounds to entrance an impressionable ten-year-old. Japanese candy had been one of my favorites. Their sugar industry puts American confectioneries to shame.

As a child, I'd come to respect the Japanese people and, as I grew older, I understood how they'd become such a power prior to the Second World War. They could be an intense population, working hard in school and at work, but they could also be a deeply caring people. They were people who would take in a Gaijin mother and her son and treat them as part of the family.

But there was no time for a stroll down memory lane on this trip. With my day job secured upon landing in Tokyo, my mind switched gears to what lay ahead. I scrolled through

Edgar Matsuyama's dossier as the hotel shuttle did its best to wind through the packed Tokyo traffic.

Edgar Matsuyama. 27 years of age.

Edgar was raised in a mixed household consisting of an American mother and a Japanese engineer father. Young Edgar had a pleasant only-child upbringing and enjoyed the benefits of a hardworking Japanese father and a doting mother. Avery had included pictures of Edgar as an awkward seventh grader buried in a class photo.

Fast forward two years and Edgar had long hair and sported a nose ring, the start of his rebellious streak. Edgar played soccer, had been in the drama club and played with the band, drums and keyboard. That had led him to founding the DJ club in his senior year of high school.

There he was in a picture with four of his cohorts, looking tough over a secondhand set of turntables and speakers.

Edgar Matsuyama, petty criminal.

At age 19, he had been nabbed by the Arizona State University police in a well-orchestrated drug raid. It was a relatively minor thing for Edgar. A few bags of weed. But the next year, Edgar had dropped out of school completely, and that's when his criminal behavior really picked up.

Vagrancy in Dallas.

Theft in Birmingham.

Loitering in New York City.

And then, finally, assault in Seattle.

That last charge had put Edgar in jail for a solid six months. He'd come out seemingly a reformed man, serious about life on the outside. He'd been released early for good behavior. He even received a personal recommendation from the prison counselor, who said that Edgar's music classes had been a big hit with the inmates.

So what went wrong?

Edgar's associates in jail included a who's who of the West

Coast criminal underground. In exchange for their protection, Edgar had agreed to perform certain tasks outside the prison walls. He reassimilated into civilian life. He took up a job at a music store in downtown Seattle. That job soon led to gigs as a DJ in small and medium-sized clubs.

Edgar stayed off the police blotter, not quite the model citizen, but something close to it. There were no new mug shots in the dossier, but there were plenty of CCTV snapshots acquired by the wily Avery.

Edgar walking into a bank.

Edgar taking the bus home.

Edgar meeting his friends in a dimly lit corner of the city.

The rest of the neatly-typed file included the apartment he kept in Tokyo, the clubs he typically worked while in town, and even his favorite restaurants. Avery had been thorough. I liked that about her.

I slipped the cell phone back in my pocket and closed my eyes. If you've never tried visualization, you should. It's a handy tool to get you ready for a football game, or a conversation with your son. That day when I closed my eyes, all I could visualize was me putting a knife through Edgar Matsuyama's heart.

THE LION HUNTS AT NIGHT

The streets of Tokyo after the sun goes down. Neon lights in high gear. Flashy billboards splashed in high definition on every side of the road. Crowds of Japanese youth mingling, chatting, taking selfies, playing games on their cell phones. A cultural playground for a society lost in the psychotic years after the Big War, and found again in the Age of Tech.

Pretty much the same as when I used to come with my Navy buddies up from Yokosuka Naval Base. Four headstrong SEALs loaded with whatever booze the base package store had on sale - ready to party. The only difference now was that technology had kicked the advertisements into HD warp speed, and everyone and their mother held a cellphone like it was some handheld life support device. Technology flashed all around me as I walked down the street smoking a cigarette, you know, to fit in. I could barely keep up with all the visual stimulation surrounding me, commanding my attention.

You'd think that I'd stand out, a six and a half foot tall American in the middle of a Japanese horde, but there were plenty of other foreigners. I heard snippets of Australian-accented English, deep, guttural German, and the quick clip of Russian from a trio of long-legged models.

Tokyo is very much an international hub, and within that hub are districts. If you were in town to have a few drinks, to dance, to get away from the real world, the Roppongi district is Disneyland for adults. Bars and dance clubs open at dusk and close at dawn.

I took my time getting to my final destination. I'd already been by Edgar's apartment. It was just where Avery said it was, and I'd even seen the DJ's head in the window. I considered barging in and taking care of him then and there, but that was too easy, too quick.

Edgar Matsuyama deserved better. He deserved my full and undivided attention.

I stepped into a small sushi joint, the kind with a conveyor belt and bar. I took a seat between two middle-aged men. They were chatting over beers and plates of sashimi, and didn't even acknowledge my presence when I sat down between them.

Twenty-eight minutes later, I was up and moving again. I could feel the tempo on the streets rising. A television mounted above the door of one particular bar showed the latest UFC fight; two men bashing each other's brains in. Modern day gladiators.

I slipped into one club and then another, each time paying the $20 cover charge, and wandering through the crowd to find a quiet corner to sip my beer. And wait.

The third club was where I found him. It was the most exclusive of all. Not only did I have to pay a $100 cover, I had to slip the bouncer another $200 to get in, much to the annoyance of those in the queue that snaked around the corner.

Before I even stepped through the door, I felt the bass rattling my chestplate. The sound was deep and penetrating, but not uncomfortable. It was like the depths of the earth calling me home. As a connoisseur of a wide variety of music, I understood the allure, and I savored the feeling as I walked inside the club. The hypnotic bass undertones – the human heartbeat amplified to the point of distraction; melodic treble; and vocals dancing on the edges. And yet, nothing too harsh. Something just right for the fans in their various inebriated states.

Edgar Matsuyama garnered quite a crowd. I estimated a thousand party-goers inside, and many more clambering to gain entrance. It was no wonder he made ten grand per night.

Maybe he should have stuck to that line of work. Maybe he should have gotten a clue.

It wasn't until I'd gotten a drink and settled into a small alcove just off the stage that Edgar made his grand entrance. He had a neon yellow, flat-billed baseball cap on backwards. He'd changed from the all black attire he'd been wearing on that plane. Now it was bright red Adidas, stark white jeans, and no shirt. The crowd erupted as he walked out whirling a towel over his head.

The bass intensified. Edgar was oblivious to my presence. Without a word, he dove into his well-rehearsed routine. I had to give it to him, he was good. Not the best, and too bad for him – he'd never have time to become the best.

* * *

I LEFT HALFWAY THROUGH HIS PERFORMANCE. THERE WERE final preparations to be made.

Besides, I knew exactly when he was leaving. Edgar was predictable like that, and it didn't hurt that the club's program said he would be DJing until four in the morning. That gave me plenty of time to do what I needed to do.

Avery's dossier said that Edgar always took a girl home.

He never left with them, but I'd seen him slip a girl in the front row a notecard with a pill taped to the back. She hadn't hesitated, popping the pill in her mouth and slipping the card into her bra.

Another quirk of Edgar's was that he never took his conquests back to his apartment. That was his safe place. Edgar Matsuyama kept a tidy home. He preferred instead to pick some out-of-the-way hotel room. That's where Avery had picked up on his trail. He used the same alias every time he came to Tokyo: Tyler Goldsmith.

Tyler Goldsmith was scheduled to arrive at his hotel room at approximately 5:15 in the morning. He'd been kind enough to alert the hotel to that fact. Too bad for him he would never make it.

Edgar Matsuyama, aka Tyler Goldsmith, walked the streets of Tokyo alone, away from Roppongi, and into my waiting hands. I don't know if it was caution or just the need to get away from it all, but Edgar liked to pick a hotel off the beaten path, away from the growing number of cameras dotting the Tokyo streets.

That was fine with me.

I spotted him ten blocks away from the hotel and tailed him the entire way. There were plenty of places to hide, and he never once looked back, supremely confident of the safety of a Japanese city. Theft and murder are virtually non-existent in this part of town. It was a strange aspect of Japanese society that it felt more like a totalitarian state, but it served my needs perfectly.

When he turned down the last alley to the back entrance of the hotel, I rushed to catch up. He was steps away from the door.

"Hey, Edgar," I slurred dramatically.

He turned. I saw the look of annoyance and a lack of recognition.

"Hey, it's my famous DJ friend. Do you remember me?"

"No, sorry man. I've gotta—"

"No, we met earlier, remember?"

He squinted in the dim light as I came closer, completely oblivious to the danger.

"Yeah, wait, I do know you. From the club?"

"No, no. You were in first class; I was in a uniform?"

I was close enough now to see that his pupils were dilated. He was on some drug but far from incapacitated.

"Oh yeah, yeah," he said amiably, although by the tone of his voice, I could tell he didn't recognize me. You'd think a man who had spent time in prison would remember every face that he saw - especially a man who'd chosen the path of Edgar Matsuyama.

"Yeah," I said, "I was going to my place, and I saw you. Thought I'd say hello."

"Well, that's cool man. I appreciate it."

I put my arm around him like we were best friends. He didn't even flinch. It was so easy. I felt the heat of his skin under my forearm.

"We should get a drink, man. Let's talk," I said.

"That'd be great, but," pointing to the hotel door, "I've got a friend waiting."

"Oh, a friend," I said. "Guy or girl?"

"A girl," he said with a chuckle.

"Hey, listen, I'm not judging," I said. "It's cool either way. Well, hey, how about a rain check?"

"Yeah, sure, no problem," he said, trying to ease away from my grip, but I held on.

I detected the first hint of panic, and I lapped it up like a Labrador attacking a raw steak.

"Listen, man, I've gotta go," he said again. "Do you mind?"

"Sure, sure," I replied, still holding on. Then I looked

straight into his eyes, foreheads almost touching, and started to squeeze. He squirmed under my grip, clawed at my arms.

"Hey, what are you doing?"

"You owe me, Edgar." Not a trace of slur.

"What do you—?" His last words came out in a gasp as I crushed his larynx with my forearm, just hard enough so he couldn't scream out.

It was so tempting to take him to some dark place and cut him apart, piece by piece, but I was no butcher. Besides, I'm not some sicko. I was there to do a job - a job that I'd thought about for the last five years. A job that I thought about every time Avery sent me an update on Edgar Matsuyama's dossier. I knew Edgar Matsuyama better than Edgar knew himself. To the world, he was a successful DJ who was on his way to playing packed festivals and sold out shows. But I knew the other Edgar, the one hidden from plain sight, the one who had torn my world apart, the world that had almost cast me to the grave.

The licking light of flame from Bangkok entered my mind, and I knew that Edgar's body would have been a fitting donation. But this was Tokyo, not the slums of Thailand. Not as easy to get away with arson here.

So I looked at Edgar one last time. I kissed him on the forehead as his eyes bulged. Then I tightened my grip, twisted, and snapped his spine in two.

DEEP THOUGHTS WITH TOM GREER

I know, I know. You've got questions.

What did I do with the body?

Why am I killing these people?

Am I going to get away with it?

Let's start with the first question: disposing of the body of Edgar Matsuyama.

Like I mentioned before, I know Tokyo, and my preparations early in the day were all about making sure nothing had changed with my disposal methods. I didn't get fancy, and I wasn't trying to send a message. In fact, alerting anyone to what had happened to Matsuyama was the last thing I wanted.

So here's what I did. I took a little trip. My rental car was a block away from the crime scene. I tossed Edgar's lifeless body in the trunk and was on my way. My voyage took me a leisurely two hours to get to the Marine outpost at the base of Mount Fuji. It was named Camp Fuji.

I'd done some training there years before, and I'd always found the Marines accommodating, especially if we let them tag along and blow through some of our ammo. And this day was no different. I even recognized the Marine at the gate.

"Good morning, Corporal," I said as I pulled up, my military ID card in hand.

"Well if it isn't the scum of the Navy," the Marine said with a crooked smile, his cheek stuffed with chewing tobacco. He stepped out of the guard shack and offered his hand. "It's good to see you, Tom."

If I hadn't become a SEAL, I probably would have been a Marine. There was something about the way they protected their own. Even the skinny ones were as tough as nails when they got into a scrap.

"Out to run the trails again?" he asked.

"I've gotta work off last night's booze."

"Let me guess, Roppongi?"

"That's the poison."

"Well, should be a perfect morning for a run. As long as you stick to your usual route, you'll be clear of any live fire. Besides it's a light day today, it being Sunday and all."

"Now Corporal," I said, "you're not telling me that the United States Marine Corps, the world's most elite fighting force, is taking a day off?"

The corporal let go of my hand. "Somebody's got to go to church and pray for the souls of you SEAL heathens. Lord knows, you ain't doing it."

We both smiled at each other. The Navy and Marine Corps would go on ribbing each other until time stopped.

The corporal waved me through. "Live long and prosper, my friend."

I set out slowly toward a quiet part of the base where I was privileged to have access. Small favors do wonders. The range was rarely used, and would be the final rest stop for my buddy Edgar Matsuyama. The corporal was right. There were no surprise encounters along the way.

Three hours later, I left through the same gate, covered in sweat, dirt, and volcanic dust. It had taken me ten minutes to bury Edgar's body, courtesy of the bulldozer sitting idle, waiting for the combat engineers to keep filling the live fire range. No one would care that there was freshly moved earth. A lance corporal would probably assume that another lance corporal had done it. It would be 50 years before they found the body, and by then, no one would care that there was ever a piece of bacteria called Edgar Matsuyama. So it was with supreme confidence that I waved goodbye to the new guard on post and headed back to Tokyo.

Nighty night, Edgar. Have a nice sleep.

So there you go. There's my story about what happened to that worthless carcass.

* * *

I ALMOST FORGOT! THERE WERE TWO MORE QUESTIONS: 1) Why was I doing this, and 2) would I get away with it?

You know what? I can't give you both answers at once. And if I give you too much of one answer, you'll leave without enough of the other. I know, it sounds strange. But I need to do this my way. You'll get your answers, I promise. In the meantime, feel free to speculate.

Is your mind creeping back to the psychopath hypothesis? I don't blame you if it is. Any casual observer to my story would fall on to the same conclusion. As I said, you're free to speculate. But think on this: If your psychopath hypothesis is correct, how then do you account for my father, Avery, Agent Baxter, and the debt I left behind? How do they all tie together? How do they become one?

So continue on, my friend. Off we go on another adventure. Where the path leads, only I know. Let's take the next step together, side by side. As friends maybe? We'll talk about that soon.

Let's move along.

There are two things you need to know: How it begins, and how it ends.

HOW IT BEGINS

Admit it. Some part of you wants to see me kill again. It's okay, you don't have to deny it. Before we jump into the good stuff though, I figured you might need an explanation. You want me to shed a little light onto why Tom Greer, Jr. became a killer. It wasn't by accident. Maybe you picked up on the little comment about me going into my father's profession. Well, I did. But at this point, you don't need to know the hairy details. It's enough to say that the United States government made me a killer. Not a cold-blooded killer, but a thinking, breathing, feeling killer. The first time I ever killed a man, I threw up an hour later. I don't know why. I just did.

Sometimes I think it was my 21st century self shedding the civilized me. Like a drug user purging the poisons from his body, I had to purge mine.

I want you to understand the difference between people like me and human beings who would never kill a gnat. From a young age, we've all been told that harming another person is bad.

"Don't hit that person, little Johnny."

"Don't push back, little Susie."

Lately, instead of fistfights in the schoolyard, we have sneaky attacks on social media.

I remember the first fight I ever got in. It was second grade. The kid was a full foot taller than me. I was small at the time. Thank God for growth spurts. We lived on the naval base in Yokosuka, Japan, and I walked to and from the school every day.

For some reason, this kid had singled me out. He picked me, quiet Tommy Greer, out of the crowd, to become his personal whipping boy. You'd think that because my father was who he was that I would fight back, but you have to understand that I had the pressures of society and the values of my mother deeply embedded in my brain.

It was bad to fight. It was bad to hurt others.

I did well in school, kept my head down and had few friends.

But this bully was relentless. He teased me in class. He followed me home from school, heckling me the entire way. He pushed me down and knocked my books away.

Second grade. And it was all done outside the view of teachers and parents. I wasn't a tattletale. Even at that young age, I knew something was wrong about running to the authorities. Maybe I had some Mafia DNA from my mother's side of the family in me.

Either way, it went on for weeks, and I don't know if much would have changed if it hadn't been for the one day that I came home with my brand-new jeans scuffed with green from my latest fall, my eyes rimmed in red. My loving mother confronted me, and when she did, the emotions flooded forth.

I told her everything. I told her about the boy. I told her about how it made me feel. I told her that I wanted to leave school. I wanted us to move back to the United States.

She listened through it all, and then she hugged me. I still remember that hug, I didn't want her to let go. Then she pulled me back at arm's length and looked me straight in the eye.

She said, "Tommy, the next time that bully pushes you down, you fight back."

I remember protesting, "But I'll get in trouble. You'll get mad."

Her eyes were full of promise. "I will not get mad. You hit him, son. You hit him so hard that he never forgets you. Do you understand me?"

I didn't have the words, so I just nodded.

She gave me another hug, and off I went to do my homework.

It didn't take long. Two days later, I was walking home on a cool sunny day when the bully made his move. I had almost forgotten about the conversation with my mother. A day in the life of a second grader will do that. Kids tend to forget, but all the fear and lost sleep came back as soon as I heard his voice.

The other kids scattered at his approach. He towered over all of us. A second grade giant.

I kept walking, thinking that maybe I could avoid him, but he called out to me.

"Tommy, Tommy wants his mommy."

If only I'd had the clever vocabulary that I do now. I kept walking.

"Are you going to see your mommy, Tommy?"

There were giggles all around, and still I kept walking. Apparently, he wanted my attention because I felt him grab my backpack and yank me back harshly. It was strong enough that I was pulled to the ground, banging my tailbone painfully.

But that pain gave me focus. The second grade me looked

up at that bully, his whitewashed hair shining in the sunlight, eyes blazing, grin radiating superiority for his audience to see. That's when I learned another lesson: *Never let your enemy know you're coming.*

I sprang from the ground much too fast for him to recover. He was back peddling as I jumped on top of him. He probably could have thrown me off because of my size, but instead, he fell backwards, flat as a pancake.

Every bit of rage and pain flowed through me, and my tiny hands pummeled away. I hit him in the chest and in the face, screaming all the way. I don't remember if he tried to hit back, my eyes were blurred with tears. The world had gone silent, save for my firehouse of anger. It felt like hours at the time, but I'm sure it was less than 30 seconds.

The bully got up and ran, he ran so fast that he was soon out of sight. As the adrenaline rushed through my body and the children whispered around me, I got to my feet, refusing to dust myself off. I left my first battlefield and walked home to my mother.

She knew what was going to happen. She was waiting just inside the front door. I remember her eyes; there was concern there and a hint of sadness. She smiled grimly.

"What happened, son?"

"I..."

"It's okay. You can tell me."

"He wouldn't leave me alone so I jumped on him and I beat him up."

She knelt down to look in my eyes, on my level. "Are you okay?" she asked. I nodded. "Is the other boy hurt?"

"I don't know, he ran home."

That's when she enveloped me with her hug. "I'm proud of you," she said.

I lost myself to the sobs.

That's not the end of the story. You see, I learned another valuable lesson out of my second grade encounter.

That bully didn't show up for school the next day. No, he didn't have a smashed face or a broken arm, he probably just complained about not feeling well. But when he did come to school, things were different. In a way that I've seen male children do time and time again, we somehow reconciled. There were no apologies, just the silent assent that I was his equal.

After that day, we became fast friends. I helped him with his school work, and he was my constant companion.

Life went on, but I never forgot the lesson.

Here we go again. You're wondering if there's a point to my story. I promise you there is.

That was one of only two fights I ever got into as a kid. Living on base was pretty tame and safe for the dependents of service members. I don't have tales of roving gangs coming to find the SEAL hero's son.

What I learned in that episode, and many times throughout my life, is that a normal human being will go to great lengths to avoid violence. How many mothers and fathers have stood with a gun in their hand as an intruder entered their home and threatened their children, only to be left robbed or worse? They had the ability. They'd gone to the range. They had a weapon in hand, and yet they did nothing.

When did we as human beings begin to think that it was okay not to protect ourselves? When did we start thinking that it was okay to let murderers off the hook, to let rapists live out their lives without punishment?

I see where your mind's going again. You're thinking if we all wanted retribution we'd be a land of vigilantes, vendettas would span the globe, and no one would get a night's sleep. It's a good thing for government, isn't it? It's a good thing that we have politicians to tell us what we should and should not do. What we should and should not think. How we should and should not live.

But here's the rub, my friend: I learned a long time ago that life isn't fair. It's a series of adventures, sometimes grand and sometimes scary. What it all comes down to is the person you want to be. Do you want to be one of the sheep or do you want to be one of the lions?

You don't have to be a gun-toting patriot to be a lion. Some of the bravest people I've ever seen were women who stood toe-to-toe with gang members, demanding them to leave the neighborhood, to leave their child's life alone.

So I guess what I'm saying is: Stand up for something. Stand up for anything. Be brave, have courage in spite of your fear. We all walk different paths, but at the end of the day, how do you want your story to be written?

With me, it's different. I know who I am. I know what I must do.

So I guess when it comes down to it, for me this is a story about revenge, plain and simple. I need to right a wrong. A wrong that the police could not right. A wrong that the government could not fix, but a wrong that would not be forgotten.

So here we go, my friend. Are you ready? Do you want to plunge deeper into my darkness? Do you want to see how I stand up to the shadows and make *them* fear *me*?

If you don't, there's the door. If you do, read on, dear friend. It's time to get down to business.

HOW IT ENDS

My daughter was born four weeks premature. We called her our miracle baby. We loved that miracle baby so much that less than a year later, our son was born. Irish twins.

My life changed when those beautiful babies came into my world. They were the final nail in the coffin of my Navy career, the best choice I ever made.

We lived a good life after that, a great life. I became a full-time pilot, and our small family used the perks of my airline job. We traveled as a team, the Greer Four. Beaches in Tahiti, mountains in Colorado. Home in Nashville.

My wife and I made a good team. We balanced each other out. Sometimes, she was the strong hand, and sometimes I was the axe wielder. We loved those kids unconditionally. There wasn't a day that went by in their young lives that they didn't get a hug and a kiss from at least one of us.

My daughter, Ella, was shy but ever-observant. She loved her daddy, and daddy loved her. I remember the small things, like when she didn't want me to braid her hair anymore, when only mommy could do that because I would leave tangles or random threads of hair that she didn't want to show at school. That one hurt more than I liked to admit. There were still the hugs, the snuggles before bedtime. She was my little angel, the second mother to her younger brother.

Caleb was precocious in all the right ways, questioning why certain rules were in place, poking and prodding to find out how the world worked. Why clouds floated overhead. How a golf ball picked up spin as it rocketed off a driver. When the world would evolve into something new. We wore out the Internet together finding answers to his endless questions.

Ella and Caleb fought occasionally, like all brothers and sisters do as young children. But the next moment, they begged to sleep in the same room on weekends. My wife and I pretended we didn't hear their whispers late into the night. Their bond was strong.

As single digits morphed into teenage years, Ella blossomed into a beautiful young woman. Caleb became a soccer player, a popular kid, although he never wore that on his sleeve.

The only time he ever got in a fight in school was when he came to the defense of a new kid who was being picked on. We had to have a talk about that one. Maybe a head-butt into the bridge of a kid's nose wasn't the best reciprocal response for stuffing someone in a locker. But what do you expect from a son who's raised by a Navy SEAL father?

Before we knew it, Ella was in college, eighteen and studying at UTC. That's the University of Tennessee at Chattanooga, for all you non-Tennesseans. She loved the outdoors and was planning on being an English major. From the age of six, we rarely saw Ella without a book in her hands.

Caleb was on the fence. He'd received scholarship offers to play soccer in many of the country's top schools, but there had been one offer he couldn't ignore. The University of

Tennessee Chattanooga, where his big sister was, made a humble offer and one that I'm sure he would've accepted to be near his big sister.

So like I said, they were good kids. They rarely got in trouble. We gave them everything as long as they earned it. We were the perfect family. I loved my wife and she me, and together we lorded over our awesome family, the King and Queen of some fairytale story.

So why wouldn't we send them overseas? Why wouldn't we let them take advantage of my status as an airline pilot? Free tickets, elite class. We called it "first class" back then. They wanted to go to Tokyo together, to see their favorite up and coming DJ. Yeah, a DJ by the name of Edgar Matsuyama.

The siren's call.

My children went to him. How were we supposed to know he wasn't just a performer? We didn't know what lurked beneath his cool exterior. Sweet Ella and sporty Caleb were entranced by Matsuyama's show. What they didn't know, was that Matsuyama was a talent scout. Before my children left Tokyo, they were invited by Matsuyama to a casual dinner with his friend, Ning Lee. Yeah, that's Target Number Three.

Together, Matsuyama and Lee put on all the right moves. They flattered and enticed, and when Ella and Caleb came home, they couldn't stop talking about the dynamic duo in Tokyo.

Ella told me that Lee was developing a platform that would take his friend Matsuyama from playing dingy bars to selling out stadiums. They said they needed scouts in America, loyal fans who could help them spread the news, help them get more followers on social media.

Caleb said that Lee was a soccer player too, that he'd invited Caleb to take a summer internship and that his company even had its own soccer team.

My wife and I were proud of them, that they'd gone off on

an adventure and came back with real world opportunity. At least, that's what we thought.

One month later, they met Matsuyama and Lee in Los Angeles. Again, courtesy of my free tickets. I asked them if they wanted me to go along for moral support, but really I was curious. Ella had spoken up and said that they could take care of themselves.

Caleb and Ella came back more excited than before.

They'd seen the written offer. They were both being offered positions for the summer. They could take internships from June to August and come back to UTC together, a college sophomore and freshman head and heels above their peers.

I was excited for them. Why wouldn't I be? Every father wants his children to succeed. We wanted them to have opportunities. Why would I look into the company past a cursory examination online? They were real companies. These were real people.

Why didn't I do more digging?

It was the summer trip when things went wrong.

There was a teary goodbye at the Nashville airport. They had never been away from us for more than a week at a time, minus Ella's time in college. I was going to try to get to Tokyo for work, but even that was no guarantee. I'm not ashamed to say that I was crying right there with my wife as we waved goodbye. Our two grown children, adults in many ways, but always innocent babies in our eyes.

It was two weeks later that Ella called, frantic and out of breath. She hadn't seen Caleb in three days. He'd taken a trip with some of his company friends; she thought they'd gone to Mount Fuji or somewhere near there. It was supposed to be only a day trip. I questioned her at length and found out that Caleb's friends had already returned. They said he'd met a girl and that he'd be back in Tokyo by week's end.

I told Ella to relax, and that everything would be okay. I tried calling Caleb's cell phone for the rest of the day, but there was no answer. I left a total of seven messages. Seven. That number seems to be a theme in my life.

I told my wife that I would take care of it, that I would make sure both of the children were safe. I failed.

The next time I called Ella, there was no answer. My wife asked me how everything was going. I lied. I told her that the children were fine, but something deep inside me had triggered a systematic panic in my body.

I never got to talk to my children again. Never got to tell them that I loved them. I never got to see their smiles. I never got to hold them and tell them that everything would be okay. There were so many things I never got to do.

There were investigations and even the FBI got involved. But it wasn't until I contacted one of my old SEAL buddies, a grizzled veteran who had served under my father, that we found out the truth.

This particular SEAL had spent his time after leaving the Navy tracking down children and adults who had been swallowed by the human trafficking system. I hadn't wanted to make that call because deep down I knew the truth. I knew what had happened, but my friend confirmed it anyway.

My sweet Ella and my wonderful Caleb had taken the bait: hook, line and sinker.

My friend found Ella's body 62 days later during a clandestine raid of a sheik's mansion in Yemen. I couldn't look at the pictures, even though my friend had been kind enough to keep us from seeing the worst.

Caleb's remains were found ten months later. Ten months, almost exactly how much younger he was than his sister. My SEAL friend told me that Caleb had been sold to a Russian Politburo member with very specific tastes. I didn't need to know more.

They say few marriages survive the death of a child. Now imagine what happens when you lose two of your children. My wife never once blamed me, and I'm proud to say that she was the strong one. She was the one that somehow moved on.

I couldn't let it go.

I needed revenge.

And so I tracked them down with Avery's help. One by one, from that first man that I'd killed and set on fire. He was a low-level contact, the one who'd orchestrated the final kidnapping of both Ella and Caleb. A common thug.

I wanted all of it burned to the ground. The organization that snuffed out the life of my two beautiful children and had almost claimed me. The organization that fed the insatiable appetite of their twisted clients, and then used that money to invest in real world companies you probably frequent on a weekly basis. A seven-headed monster, the bane of my life.

The killer of my children.

TURBULENCE

Two down, five to go.

That thought swirled in my head as I surrendered to the delicious escape of sleep. Dreams had never plagued me. Maybe it was because I had been trained to dissect what was real and what was not. Whatever the cause, demons cloaked in black were not what kept me up at night. Even through my deepest pain I'd been allowed the gift of slumber as if some universal power deemed it necessary for my body and mind to maintain their strength.

But that night in Tokyo, much like the one in Bangkok, I did not exalt in the killings like you might think. I was not a cold-blooded murderer, despite what the law might say. And yet, sleep came easily, unbidden but completely welcome - a warm blanket cast over me as my mind drifted away on soothing lullabies.

I snapped awake at 4:47am precisely. I knew because my head was turned to face the green glow of the clock. I hadn't set an alarm, and the depth of my slumber surprised me. I'm a sound sleeper, but I happen to have the uncanny knack of doing so while remaining alert. It's what folks mean when they talk about sleeping with one eye open. Every pin drop is analyzed by my reptilian brain and either wakes me or deems the intrusion non-threatening. It had kept me alive on more than one occasion.

But it wasn't my alarm blaring, it was my phone ringing. The clock ticked over.

4:48am Tokyo time.

I grabbed the phone. It was Avery.

My stomach immediately tightened as I answered the call.

"Is everything okay?" I asked.

"What?"

"I said is everything okay?"

"Were you asleep?" Avery asked.

"Of course I was asleep, it's 4:45 in the morning."

"Oh, sorry. I wasn't paying attention."

I took a deep breath trying to reclaim the calm I'd had minutes before. *Focus on the task at hand.*

"Any red flags with our friend?" I asked, meaning Matsuyama.

"Nothing yet."

"Good, keep me posted."

"Did you make sure...?" Avery began.

"Make sure of what? Oh yeah, that. Yeah, it was taken care of."

Avery didn't need to know the details. She wanted to think that she was some kind of super spy, my hardcore side-kick, but she'd never seen death up close. I hadn't dragged her into the scenario, but I sure as hell didn't want to be the one to taint her world outlook.

She was smart. She could figure it out herself but I was pretty sure she'd have the exact same reaction that any normal human being would have if she saw what I'd done: horror. She'd look at me like a monster. The way you're looking at me now. And while I shouldn't have cared, I somehow always rationalized her involvement. I think Avery knew what she had gotten into. To me, she was still a child in many ways, becoming my own kin as the days went by.

"Do you need something Avery? Besides the satisfaction of ruining my sleep?"

She answered through a mouthful of crunching cereal. "I just thought you'd want to know about Baxter."

"What about him?"

"I've been tracking him all over Tokyo." For a moment I thought she was going to say that he had been following me. "He hasn't stopped since before midnight. He's been north, south, east and west. It's actually pretty impressive."

"Tell me what he's doing."

"He stopped at three warehouses down at the docks, two private helipads, got some coffee at about 3:00am."

I rubbed my eyes. "I didn't ask where he'd been. I asked, what's he doing?"

"Whatever, Captain Grumpypants. He's just taking notes. Drives up to a building and looks around for a little bit. I mean I can't see everything. Cameras aren't covering every square inch of Tokyo, but it looks like he's just sort of snooping around."

"In other words, he's doing what the FBI sent him to do."

"Sure, I guess," Avery said. "But it seems kind of strange, doesn't it? Why didn't he do that during the day when there were tons of people out?"

"Maybe he's a night owl. I'm sure there're plenty of those in his profession. Just keep tracking him. I'm meeting him for lunch so maybe I'll ask him what he did tonight."

"You mean this morning," Avery corrected.

"What?"

"You said 'tonight'. Technically he was working this morning."

Avery had that youthful way of correcting the smallest

details that most people didn't care about. I was used to it by now.

"How are we on the next trip?" I asked.

There was no way I was getting back to sleep. Once I was up, I was up. With the phone stilled glued to my ear, I slid out of bed, my bare feet touching the carpet, and I immediately went into my morning stretching routine. There was a time in my early days as a SEAL, when stepping out of bed was as easy as a stroll on the beach. Now the aches and pains of an aging body assaulted my hips, my right knee, and a left ankle I'd shattered on a mission in the Ukraine.

"Everything looks good on my end," she said. She ran through some mundane details. I was only half-listening, willing my body to comply. I was just getting to my quads when I realized that Avery had stopped talking. I looked at my phone to see if I'd lost the connection. No, she was still there.

"Avery?"

"Tom, there's something you have to see."

My stretching routine forgotten, I reached across the bed and grabbed my laptop. It took a few moments for the connection to grab hold and a few more as I typed in three separate passwords until I was finally inside Avery's system. What appeared to be a live camera feed materialized onto my screen.

"What am I looking at?"

Then it hit me like a dose of ice water on the back. I'd been outside the exact same building the morning before. Edgar Matsuyama's apartment complex.

And standing outside in clear view of the close-circuit television system was Agent Baxter, scribbling in a notebook.

MORE TURBULENCE, COURTESY OF NED BAXTER

"Avery, what is he doing there?" I said slowly.

"I don't know. I'll have to go back and cross reference his other stops. Maybe there's a pattern or something... I mean, I don't want to say that he's *on to us*..."

The funny thing was that there was no panic in Avery's voice. But I thought I did detect something that concerned me: excitement.

I watched on my computer screen as agent Baxter jotted what was probably his doodle shorthand.

Maybe it was nothing. Maybe it's just a coincidence, I told myself.

No, that was impossible. Tokyo was a big town, too big for this blatant coincidence.

The seconds ticked by and, finally, Baxter left.

Avery shuffled the view to another camera. Baxter getting in the car. Baxter driving away.

"What do you think it means?" Avery asked.

"I don't know, but we need to find out soon."

* * *

I met Baxter later that afternoon at the departure lounge in the Tokyo airport. He looked no worse for wear. No sign of his predawn wanderings. If he suspected me of anything, he didn't show it. Once again, I was left in the dark with this mysterious FBI agent.

There are no such things as coincidences, I told myself. But then again, that's a lie. We run into coincidences every day, but this, *this* was too much.

"Hey, Ned. How was your stay in Tokyo?" I asked him.

"Oh, not bad. Had some sushi you can't get in the States. My quarters were a little cramped, but hey, that's Japan, right?" I nodded, almost pushing past the small talk, but caution held me back. "What about you?" Baxter asked, "Pleasant stay?"

"Caught up on some rest and reading. All in all, not too bad. I tried to call you earlier. Thought maybe we could grab some lunch."

"Yeah. Sorry about that. I was getting work done," Baxter said, not a hint of deception on his face.

"Anything I can help with?" I asked.

"No, just busy work."

Busy work my ass, I thought.

I had to figure out a way to find out the truth. How were Edgar Matsuyama and Agent Baxter linked? *It can't be me*, I told myself. I had always been careful and Avery, well, she was one of the best.

"You know," he said, "now that you mention it, I do have a question."

"Shoot," I said, plopping my bag on the floor and taking a seat next him.

Baxter leaned closer, almost conspiratorially and said, "I probably shouldn't tell you this, but there was a man on your last flight..." He looked around again. "A guy the FBI's been tracking for close to a year."

"Really? You don't say." The words came out of my mouth, but my insides flipped turns. "Who was it?"

The FBI agent stared stone-faced. "Well, you had contact with him, as a matter of fact."

Here it comes, the hammer crashing down. FBI agents swarming the airport. Would I go down fighting? Not a chance.

You see, that's what a psychopath would do.

"Really?" I said, feigning as much incredulity as a plant in a magic show audience. "Just curious, I mean, I make contact with so many folks. Who was it, Ned?"

He pursed his lips and narrowed his eyes, as if I'd just asked him the answer to a million-dollar trivia question. For his life, he wasn't about to give me anything, as this was his plan, stringing me along like a lost puppy.

"Ned?" I repeated. "Earth to Ned. Who was he?"

"I shouldn't be telling you this, but considering your background," he looked around one last time to make sure nobody was listening, "You talked to him for quite some time."

I aped his squinting mannerism, as if trying desperately to recall the interaction. "I did?"

Baxter nodded. "When you came back into the main cabin; it was after you talked to me. He grabbed your arm. Remember? Asked you something about..."

"Turbulence," I said, jabbing a victorious finger at him. "He wanted to know if there was going to be any turbulence."

You cannot imagine the relief flooding through my body at that point. Baxter wasn't talking about Matsuyama. He was talking about some faceless person that I had a momentary brush with.

The agent went on to explain how this person, and he would not give me his name, was being investigated for smuggling industrial espionage through Japan and over to China. I was only half-listening as he went into his detailed description.

It was a lot to think about, especially through the mental image of Baxter standing outside of Edgar Matsuyama's apartment.

Coincidence?

You don't believe in coincidences, Tom.

KEEPING THINGS TIDY

Much to Avery's disappointment, I suggested that we lay low for a while. We compromised on a week, maybe two.

I'd be lying if I said I wasn't disappointed too. There was a reckless side of me, a ballsy run into the middle of gunfire side, that wanted to keep going, Baxter be damned. But I was only two-for-seven and a long way from my goal.

And so a week went by, and I did my best to cozy up to Agent Baxter. When we landed in Beijing, I surprised him by inviting him to share a suite. What better way to get close? "The damn thing has three bedrooms," I told him.

He declined politely saying he was happy to stay where the FBI had booked, and that he didn't want to be a burden.

Too late, Agent Baxter. You're a real drag on what I'm trying to get done.

Avery wasn't helping things. The entire two days I was in Beijing, she kept giving me status reports on Target Number Three. For nearly forty-eight hours, I was within one mile of him, but never once did I pursue. Instead, we tracked

Baxter's late-night wanderings. This time, his path and the target's didn't intersect.

* * *

THE FIRST BEIJING TRIP WENT BY, AND THEN WE TRAVELED to Seoul, Korea. By the time we got back to the States, the word 'coincidence' was once again dangling before my eyes, the carrot that the universe wanted me to take. But there would be more opportunities. I had to keep telling myself that. Avery had a firm hold on Target Number Three. Besides, it wasn't like the target was making any attempt at staying anonymous. Quite the opposite was true.

I thought about volunteering for another flight and moving up on the target list, but I quickly cast that aside. We'd made the list in that exact order for a reason. Taking it one step at a time up the ladder was the smart thing to do. But when a week had gone by, I was as ready as Avery.

I wanted blood.

* * *

"WE'RE ON A ROLL, TOM. NOBODY CAN STOP US," SHE SAID as we ate lunch at The Tavern in midtown Nashville.

She was biting into a baloney sandwich and I was picking at a salad.

"You know that thing will probably kill you," I said, pointing at her sandwich. "It's a sodium nitrate bomb with an artificial preservative fuse."

She rolled her eyes and took another chomp, and I couldn't help but laugh. Avery, so strong and resilient. But she was really just a kid. But a good kid, her heart always in the right place.

"So back to Beijing," she said as she grabbed her iced tea.

"Beijing," I repeated.

"How do you think you'll do it?"

"You know I don't like talking about that. Besides, you don't want to know."

"This isn't the little old lady next door that you're taking care of," she whispered. "This is—"

I cut her off with a hard stare. "We should not be talking about this," I said. "Not here. Let's enjoy our lunch."

"Oh, come on, Tom. You really think anyone's listening in? Baxter's in D.C. and won't be back until tomorrow. I'm pretty sure Nashville's safe for us. Unless you think the ghost of Elvis is eavesdropping on the convo."

"Look, Avery, I know you don't like lectures, so I'm saying this as much for myself as I am for you. The minute we get complacent, the minute we think we're ten steps ahead of the law—"

Again, she rolled her eyes. "I know, I know. That's when we get in trouble."

"Good, as long as we understand each other. I don't know what I would do if something happened to you."

That finally got her attention. She cocked her head as if to say, "Are you kidding with that sentimental crap?" But then her face changed. The reality of what I was telling her had finally sunk in.

She put down her sandwich and dusted her fingers over the plate. "I'm sorry, Tom. I know sometimes I might sound naïve, but I'm not. I promise. I might be young but I'm thinking about this stuff all day. I think about what would happen if they caught you, if one of them saw you coming."

"And what about you?" I said sternly. "Aren't you scared that they'll find you?"

"Maybe a little," she said, but there was a smile behind her caution. Ever the optimistic youth.

"Look, I'll stop the lecture. All I'm saying is, we need to

be extra careful. We still don't know what Baxter's doing, and we don't know why he was outside our friend's apartment in Tokyo. So let's be careful, okay?"

Avery nodded and took another hulking bite of her sandwich.

"Good, let's finish lunch and talk about the next trip to Beijing."

Avery nodded eagerly, polished off her sandwich and truffle chips in record time. We then got down to business on the way out the door.

The plan was simple, keep an eye on Baxter while getting the job done.

Easier said than done.

TARGET NUMBER THREE – THE TECHNO-GEEK

Ning Lee had the charismatic air of a nerd who'd finally found his place in the world. He was the kid that everybody used to pick on, and who was now running the show.

Good for him.

Too bad he'd made some unfortunate choices in his life. And too bad that life was about to end.

I watched him in the Starbucks vestibule, chatting with a handful of international students who'd come to Beijing for their studies. The once-obese Lee was now trim, bespectacled, and perfectly manicured, pompadour slick and stylish.

Ning Lee was the picture of privilege: an American education, a solid upper middle-class upbringing, and not a speck of gratitude for any of it. He traveled around the world, starting numerous small businesses along the way.

Technology was his bag. He started young. At only 12, he built a short-lived Facebook copycat for his 6th-grade class. Over the next ten years, he would develop a string of hits and misses. With the hits outnumbering the misses to the point where no one counted the misses at all.

And now here he was, in his native China. On paper, he was on the trip to woo investors. I had tracked him to two such meetings. The first was to pitch a crypto-currency he'd developed with a friend from India. The second, an underwater drone company.

Ning Lee had an eclectic mind. Avery had a field day dissecting his past triumphs and failures. She'd grown to respect his talent, all while tracking his underworld deeds.

You see, somewhere along the way, Ning Lee got bored. Not just bored, but greedy. He'd achieved a certain level of fame in his little bubble, which gave way to more exposure to the finer things in life, to parties, to boardrooms where he reigned like a king, and to girls galore.

At 25, Ning Lee lived the untouchable life. He became everything that is wrong with today's social media culture of anonymity: Fully-grown adults who post night and day, hiding behind cloaks of obscurity, listing scathing Yelp reviews, trolling scapegoats, all because they never once think the person they're harming would ever come looking for them.

Sorry, Mr. Lee, your privilege time card just expired.

In a blink, the coeds left the Starbucks, and my target wandered over to the cashier. He ordered in flawless Mandarin and then clicked away on his phone while he waited.

A couple minutes later, coffee in hand, Lee never once looked up from his phone. He left through the front door, and I followed shortly thereafter.

I didn't have to stay close. I had my phone out too, but I wasn't pondering the latest news or updating my social media profiles. I was watching the tracking program Avery installed. Simple, but extremely effective. All I had to do in Starbucks was get within five feet of Lee for Avery to tag his phone.

I wandered through a bustling Beijing, two sometimes

three blocks away from my target. Just another guy on his cellphone, meandering away in obscurity.

It was almost dusk. Judging by his digital agenda, we knew that he had one more meeting. I had time to kill. The last business pitch of his life was on the 48th floor of a 50-story high rise. He went in at 6:57pm and came out looking smug as ever at 8:03pm, still glued to his phone.

I stepped off when he was exactly one block away, popping off the top of my coffee mug and tossing it into a trash bin. I was careful to not let the contents slosh over the side. I had steady hands, but I was still wearing latex-lined gloves.

Half a block away, and I could now see him clearly – eyes locked on the phone in his hand, shaking his head about something. I pressed *Send* on my phone. An innocuous "miss you" shot out to Avery. That was her cue.

In a moment, within the digital compounds of Beijing, a recording started to play. After a quick blip in the video system, she was in. Avery showed me exactly how it worked. She would record exactly what the video cameras were seeing in real time, but her program would fudge the details. The perfect cover.

Lee was 20 feet away. 10 feet and still staring at his phone. Just enough traffic, just enough cover between crowds. And then a space opened up and I took it, colliding with Ning Lee at a brisk pace. My cold coffee spilled all over his chest, neck, and face.

I reared back, instantly apologetic. "Oh, I'm so sorry."

"What the hell, man?" he said in English, arms spread.

He then was more worried about his phone than anything else, and was wiping it on the back of his pants.

And that's when the first rack of pain hit him. He looked up at the sky and then at me, moaning a deep, pitiful sound.

He reached out for something, anything, but then

collapsed facedown. Somehow, he managed to roll over onto his back. His body was convulsing now, but he was quite conscious, his eyes wide and staring. Nosy pedestrians converged like a herd of locusts, chittering away. Cell phones rose like lighters at a concert, as the onlookers sought to preserve the moment in video form.

But Avery was a genius. Even now, the jammer in my pocket was masking this very spot. When the onlookers eventually went back to view their footage, they would find no pictures of the scene, no videos of Lee's final death throes. There would be no evidence of a tall man, an American maybe, in a well-tailored suit, bending down to check the dying man's pulse with a gloved hand. There would be white noise and nothing else.

Even in person, it seemed the crowd looked right through me.

I leaned down and whispered so only Ning Lee could hear. "Have fun in Hell," I said. I looked up to the crowd. "Somebody call an ambulance! I think he's having a heart attack!"

I had one hand resting on his chest, feeling the thuds from the heart inside, like it was about to burst through his chest and attack me.

And I was there, right there, when I felt that heart wind down like the blades a fan. The last beat. The last exhalation of fetid breath.

And like that, Number Three was taken care of. Four more to go.

Good night, Mr. Lee. Sweet dreams. May your soul rot in Hell.

EXPLOITING WEAKNESS

Ning Lee's death was barely a blip on the Chinese radar. Avery monitored the chatter just to make sure.

The body traveled from the hospital, then quickly to the morgue. There was no fancy entourage, which meant there was no suspicion of foul play. Because of Lee's minor celebrity status in the tech world, word got to his peers and his parents quickly.

They knew what had happened before the coroner did, at least they thought they knew.

You see, there's a wonderful thing about computerized medical records. No more having to bust into a back room to read someone's most personal details. Nowadays, if you can get in the electronic back door, you've got riches, my friend. And you don't even have to get dressed.

Ning Lee was a special case. Born with a heart defect, he'd undergone four surgeries to correct the problem. That was part of the reason he'd become so overweight as a child. His parents never wanted him to strain the expensive repair. But as he had gotten older, the medical establishment had perfected their skills. As he'd strolled through

Beijing that final time, Lee believed that his heart was impervious, a normal beating organ that could never fail him. The price of privilege is a man's unerring delusion of invincibility.

And there's a funny thing about physical shortcomings. No matter how hard you tried to cover them up, no matter how many surgeries you undertake to cover up that cleft lip or fix that scar on your left arm, the memory of it is always there. If there was one thing the heart is good at doing, it's remembering.

While Lee traipsed across the globe, I did my research. He was a challenging task. Like a medieval engineer who built the perfect castle to defend against a siege, Ning Lee strengthened his body and fortified his heart.

So my answer, when it finally did arrive, came from a small pocket of some of the world's best killers. The Israelis, for example, are cunning assassins. They are not above using chemical means to eliminate a target. Crafty devils.

After a few discreet orders and an anonymous phone call from Avery, I'd gotten what I needed - a supercharged amphetamine, chemically synthesized and molecularly merged with a "messenger" catalyst. When placed topically on human skin, preferably on sensitive skin like we have on our neck, the body's own immune system fails to register it as a foreign body, and the catalyst convinces the cells to carry it through the bloodstream, straight to the heart.

In an average human being, say a normal healthy 18-year-old, the effects would've amounted to a pretty hectic, but non-lethal, panic attack; with a racing heart and mild hyper-ventilation. In Lee's case, the chemical seeping into that most vital of organs exploited its weakness. Instead of mere manageable panic, it produced a myocardial infarction. That's a heart attack for all of you laypeople out there.

Really, I'd just done what nature would've achieved in a

few years. Only I got to look him in the eyes. And I got to whisper those final words.

When the coroner's report came back, it was just as Lee's parents suspected: Massive heart attack exacerbated by a supposedly-fixed congenital heart defect.

In a matter of hours, there was a general outpouring of support from Lee's family, his companies, his employees who exalted him to some kind of modern-day Marcus Aurelius. None of them knew the truth.

I did, and so did others. But we'll get to them soon enough.

I was so confident in being undetected that I told Avery to move up the operation on Target Number Four. I'm not sure if waiting would have helped me avoid the catastrophe looming on the horizon. Sometimes a clash is inevitable, like the universe pushing two opposing forces together for a final confrontation that can only end in annihilation.

But I'm getting ahead of myself. No need to wax poetic yet. All you need to know now was that when I left Beijing, I was riding my inner high. Ning Lee would never hurt another soul again. Quite the opposite. I imagined his soul being wracked by the barbed whip of a pit fiend.

Here's to hoping, anyway.

I'd done my duty. I'd taken out the trash. It was time to move on to Number Four.

The only problem with Number Four was that's where all the trouble began.

BAXTER

Where did we go wrong? That's always the question, right? We look back on the inexplicable - some mistake, a right turn when we should've taken a left. We explain it away as bad luck, a poorly made decision. Sometimes we can't even remember when the misstep happened.

For me, it was the fourth of seven targets, but I'll get to that in a minute.

In the afterglow of my success in Beijing, I kept my head down. I was never a partier, and despite what you might think of openly celebrating, the death of another human being is still my limit.

Don't get me wrong, I felt that same inner peace that justice had been done, a wrong righted, a smear on humanity wiped from the Earth. But I wasn't jumping up and down, buying rounds at the bar. No, I did what I always did: I planned for the next mission. Part of me wondered what I would do when it was all over, when all seven were gone and I was left with just the memory.

No time to dwell on that now.

That's like Patton thinking about what life would be like

after defeating the Germans, not that he made it that far. And now that I think about it, it's an interesting parallel. General George Patton had been bred for war. He was willing to do whatever it took to win. And in many ways, I'd been raised the same way. I enjoyed my career as a pilot, but it was a long way from jumping out of airplanes and fighting in the shadows.

But there's a deeper reason for why I felt the way I did about all this. You can judge for yourself whether it's valid.

Let me tell you a quick story. Remember what I said to Baxter when I first met him and told him about a sushi joint in Tokyo, and how I was "only in it for the noodles?"

There's a reason for that.

Some years back, I found myself in an obscure part of Tokyo eating at some high-end sushi place. Different place than the one I recommended to Baxter. This place was posh; a little something for the well-traveled businessman/adventurer looking for a something of a thrill. Leather booths. Blue mood lighting, like some forbidden den of vice. Ten kinds of Saki parlayed into as many eclectic cocktails, garnished with stuff you could only find in this part of the world.

Next to each booth was a tankful of fish darting back and forth in that oblivious way that fish do. My guide, a millionaire Japanese tech guy I'd met on a flight who'd taken a shine to me and invited me out, showed me how to order off the top of the menu in a place like this. He called the waiter over and pointed to a fish in the tank next to us.

"That one," he said in Japanese.

A moment later, an arm dangled a net into the water and scooped up his choice. The sushi chef carved a choice piece out of the critter's flesh, then *tossed it back into the tank*.

My host ate while the deformed fish swam back and forth next to us.

Needless to say, I didn't feel much like eating sushi then. And I've had a hard time rustling up a craving for it since.

Now, why the hell am I telling you any of this?

Because, friend, I know about the futility of existence for certain individuals. And when you spend your days in the presence of such futility, and even add to it, you start to develop your own rationale for continuing your *own* life. You start to think that you are that fish swimming around with a chunk of him missing. And it's all you can do to keep going. You don't know why you're doing it, but you'll be damned if you admit that it's all for nothing, or that you're doing it just so the next guy can come along and take another chunk out of you.

And so I fell back into my element. That's how it happened.

But I digress. You probably want to know about Baxter. What was he up to? Did I bump into him in Beijing?

Well I did, but not for the reason you might think.

* * *

AN HOUR AND THIRTY-FIVE MINUTES AFTER I'D KILLED Ning Lee, I was showered, changed and waiting in the hotel lobby. Agent Baxter had promised to take me on a raid, as an observer. It was a joint operation with the Chinese police, some sort of an exchange program or modern-day co-op.

When we arrived at the police station, we were each given a badge. Agent Baxter explained to the police chief that I was the official representative of the American airline industry. That wasn't exactly true but the lie rolled easily off of Baxter's tongue. The police chief was polite and respectful. He never questioned Baxter's story.

To his credit, Baxter let the Chinese take all the glory. Rather than suit up and barge in the door, we sat in a neon green delivery van that reeked of week-old cabbage. We watched as the masked Chinese forces bashed down the hotel room door. I probably would've asked the hotel manager for a key. It was a Marriott after all.

The helmet-mounted cameras gave us a fine view as the squad streamed in. I gave them a B-minus for efficiency. Eleven men streamed into the room. Eleven versus one. Well, two, if you counted the naked hooker lying next to the man, sheet pulled up over her nose.

The bloated white belly of the target shined like a kite, even through the lens of a jostling camera, but there was no fight in him. He didn't resist.

I did recognize him. The man from the plane. He'd asked me about turbulence. Who knew international criminals were so lacking in knowledge of basic aerodynamics?

Baxter nudged me, "*Now* do you recognize him?"

I told him I did. Why hadn't Baxter told me who the target was? Operational security maybe? But who was I going to tell? For a second, I worried that Baxter was toying with me, judging my reaction. But his attention was firmly glued to the monitor. He jotted notes furiously. About what, I had no idea.

My turbulence guy was handcuffed and lying face down on the hotel room bed by then. The Chinese forces didn't have to look long for what they came for: a leather briefcase, no lock. It wasn't five minutes before they were out and the video feed clicked off.

And yet, Baxter kept scribbling. I didn't want to bother him. He was clearly giving free flow to some fluid stream of thought.

But a minute went by, and then two more. The Chinese who had been manning the van had already left, gone to see the spectacle of the half-naked man being trudged out of the hotel. I waited for Baxter. But then, like anyone without something to do, I got curious.

Shifting slightly to my left, I did something I hadn't done since high school: I peeked at Baxter's notes. I mainly saw the scribbly shorthand marks of his handwriting. Then I noticed the heading: It should've been the name of the man being dragged out of the hotel.

But it wasn't. It was a name I knew. A name tattooed in my memory.

No, it can't be, I told myself. I stared harder, taking a chance that Baxter would see me peeking.

It had to be a coincidence. But I don't believe in coincidences, remember?

When I tell you that the name I saw was the name of Target Number Four, you're right in thinking that maybe we should've changed our plans. But we didn't, and that's where the story gets good.

A DAY IN THE LIFE

God, I have to pee, thought Avery Van Houten.

Her fingertips danced across the keyboard, barely able to keep up with her roving eyes. She was in the zone and had been for hours. She didn't need sleep. She was buzzing on adrenaline. The thrill of the hunt had her fully ensnared. If only it weren't for her goddamned bladder.

And thank God Tom wasn't here. The old man would have told her to take a break, get some shuteye, forget about things for a while, and no more baloney, that stuff'll kill ya. She laughed to herself. Adrenaline giggles.

She didn't realize she was making the same mistake the best of the best make. The grunt out on patrol, sleep dwindling down to a few restless catnaps each night. The entrepreneur with the world-changing idea, who'd burn the midnight oil, and pound Red Bull until the sun came up and then start again.

But this was too important to take a break. That's what she told herself. It was all too important. Facebook was blowing up with some viral thing or whatever, and she didn't give a rat's butt. For whenever something called to distract her from her holy task, or whenever the gravity of the situation felt like it was slipping, she only need to remind herself of what had happened to Tom. She only needed to reflect for a moment on his unspeakable pain.

Unspeakable. That's a Tom word for sure. The man was epic that way.

He'd only spoken of it that one time, but in that moment of weakness, his pain had transferred to her, and she had made a promise to herself that she would do anything to help. She would not rest.

They'd tried the authorities first, leaking seemingly innocuous bits of information to local police, and then the FBI. Avery had become an expert analyst into what authorities would and would not pursue.

There were two problems. One was manpower: There was only so much a limited budget could do, even with the help of technology. The second snag was the law: Much of the information they'd provided the authorities would be either inadmissible in a court of law or simply too dangerous to use, and so they'd let it go.

Their shot at being normal citizens had passed by a year and a half before. That's when their planning had begun in earnest. She'd learned a lot from Tom. Not just the way his mind calculated timelines and analyzed each bit of surveillance she provided. She learned about focus. Tom had been firmly planted in his steady Zen, while she virtually bounced in her seat those first few days, tracking down each of their targets. Tom Greer was as calm as a priest in a confessional. And she was a hummingbird on caffeine.

Over time, she'd noticed his influence breaking into her psyche. Her relationship with her parents had always been contentious, sometimes leading to screaming matches over the dining room table. Now, however, every time her mother tried to egg her on, tear apart some random detail of Avery's life, she would take a deep breath, look her mother straight in the eye, and think to herself, "*What would Tom do?*"

She looked up to the man. Not like a father or in a romantic sort of way. That would be gross, right? Tom was more like a favorite uncle, the one you can tell anything to, the one you look up to, the one who won't judge.

And so they'd become each other's sounding boards – an unlikely pair, but a fitting match. She had to laugh every so often. He'd once told her about some TV show way back in the stone age about two guys who were divorced and living as roommates. One of the guys was this anal-retentive OCD dude, and the other was a slob. Tom said he and Avery were like that. He never said which was which.

As her distended bladder screamed for relief, she scrolled through screens and open files. Everything was being recorded on remote servers in the bowels of Lithuania. She had twenty such sites, each one tagged in her memory.

Tom had been explicit on that point. There would be no paper trail. When Avery had laughed and told him that paper was as extinct as the dodo, he leveled her with that firm stare, the one that always made her listen. She'd gotten the point. The last thing she wanted to do was disappoint her friend or, even worse, let him down.

So as she monitored Target Number Four and added to the dossiers of the rest. Her feet were firmly grounded. She was equal parts invincible and light as a feather. She could flip in and out of any system without being detected.

As she worked, her mind wandered to the last killing, the only one that she'd actually seen. Tom had executed it perfectly, she thought. She'd marveled at the way he'd tracked Lee, a hunting cat stalking its prey. And when the time had come, there had been no hesitation. Zero. Zilch. The splash of coffee. The surprise on Lee's face. The collapse and the surge of the crowd.

Through it all, Avery had watched Tom's face. She would never tell Tom this, but she expected a nervous twitch, or maybe the squinted eyes of someone so focused that they could not lose. But that wasn't Tom. Even surrounded by all those people, even as he ushered in the death of their third target, Tom was calm and steady. No sea too choppy, no road too winding. He was like a robot.

She moved past the memory, and then clicked on another surveillance video and threw it in a file for Tom.

The two of them were in a groove now. Avery could almost anticipate what the old man was going to ask before he opened his mouth. Ingress and egress routes. Approximate street population at a certain time of day. The make and color of the usual vehicles on a certain block.

She'd learned so much from him. She finally took her well-earned pee break, and as she sat there, she wondered what would happen when it was all over. How could she go back to attending school, being a normal student, another blank face in the crowd? This wasn't the kind of stuff she could put on her resume. Stroll up to CIA headquarters and say, "Hey, I'm a computer genius with a history of tracking targets for assassination, want to check out my portfolio of the hapless jerks I helped a guy kill?"

She hadn't told Tom about those thoughts. Better to stay in the moment like he did. But she couldn't. Her eye was on the future now when she returned to her computer; she could picture the endless horizon, and her mind was so focused on what she could become that she didn't see the blip. At first, it was just a jittery image, and then the video feed went out altogether.

"What the hell?" she said to no one.

She clicked on a few icons and typed in a few lines of code, but nothing worked. Maybe it was just a power outage overseas. She quickly discarded that guess, but then one by one, the tabs on her browser began disappearing.

Maybe she'd accidentally triggered the shut down procedure. Later, she would blame it on her mental fatigue, going too many hours without replenishing her clarity, and her judgment drowned in pee.

She then realized what was actually happening.

She panicked, shut off her computer, and slammed the laptop shut.

Breathe, Avery, breathe, she told herself. *It's probably nothing*.

But why else would her system initiate its own lockdown?

She knew the answer, but she didn't want to admit it. Like a fighter getting knocked out for the first time, this was Avery's introductory foray into failure. She was used to winning, used to getting her own way. Now as her heart thudded in her chest, she calculated how she'd gone wrong, why the fail-safe program she'd promised Tom that she'd installed on every computer she owned had kicked into high gear.

The answer came on the heels of this thought, and it wasn't pleasant.

Someone's tracking me, she thought.

She sat there for a full thirty minutes, expecting a team of armed thugs to burst in to her apartment at any moment. She thought about calling Tom, but she didn't want to admit her mistake. After half an hour had gone by, she opened her laptop like it was made of candy glass and rebooted the system. Everything seemed in order. She didn't go back to the tainted video feed. No need to tickle that demon.

She ran a full diagnostic and found no signs of intrusion. Maybe it was all in her head. Maybe it was just a mistake, her fail-safe kicking in at the wrong time. Another ten minutes and she was ninety-eight percent sure that she was good to go.

But when she shut down her laptop again, she couldn't stop thinking about that other two percent; the possibility, however slim it might be, that someone had found her.

No, that's impossible.

She went to her kitchenette and poured a glass of water, and then another, thinking, plotting, planning. And then, like any over-confident 22-year-old, she chose a course of action.

There was no need to tell Tom.

TARGET NUMBER FOUR – THE BANKER

L ucas Laurent.

Five foot nothing.

Black hair.

Gray eyes centered over an equine nose.

Lucas Laurent. Target Number Four.

I watched him from across the street over a bowl of Indonesian street food. He was sitting in the middle, not at the head, but directly in the middle of a conference table on the other side of a vast pane of glass. The conference room and the office within belonged to one of the largest bank chains in Indonesia. Laurent had his hands steepled together to form an A with his arms. He was not facing the speaker who was gesticulating with his entire body, but it was obvious he was listening. Every once in a while, he would punctuate his own thoughts by tapping his index fingers together twice, like a mental check mark.

Finally, whatever the other man's diatribe had been about was over, and the small form of Target Number Four turned to his host. I saw his lips move, his body stock still as the words came out, like quick bursts from an automatic weapon.

Words hit the other man with jolt after jolt. It was obvious who was in charge of this conversation. Lucas Laurent, French ex-patriot, a man Avery had dubbed The Banker.

If it had been any other case, I would have been intrigued by Laurent. He was a perfect fit for a villain in a James Bond movie. His five-foot stature might have been an impediment to business in the US, but, in Asia, it didn't seem to matter. Whether it was the way he cut his black hair, like the Dutch boy on the paint can, or the way his eyes bore into subordinates and enemies alike, Laurent was a villain worth my time. Another step up the ladder.

I tossed my finished meal into the trashcan strapped to the street vendor's cart. I fished out a cigarette from my pocket and lit it, perusing a nearby newsstand. Everyone around me was digesting the day's news on their phone, and playing whatever Indonesia's latest video game craze was. Nearest to me were a bored newspaper vendor and an old man with a palsied hand who perused the periodicals.

I paid for a copy of the *New York Times* and settled in against the wooden structure of the newspaper stand. Across the way, the transparent façade of the bank's exterior allowed me to see Laurent's every move.

I was done with the first section and on to sports when Laurent left the building, but not without giving one last stern talking down to the man. Avery had pinpointed Laurent's guest as none other than the CEO of a large bank chain. The guy was reportedly worth hundreds of millions of dollars.

* * *

YOU'RE PROBABLY WONDERING SOMETHING: HOW COULD A man like that, a man who was seemingly untouchable, be dressed down by a foreigner? Let's just leave it at the fact that

Lucas Laurent, aka Target Number Four, aka The Banker, was a moneyman for some very important and influential underworld leaders. The CEO hadn't gotten to where he was on skill alone. He'd hopped, skipped, and jumped above the competition because of his connection to Laurent's bosses. Don't worry, I won't bore you with all the details.

Suffice it to say it's the same in any country around the world. Show me a successful corporation, a conglomerate who gives millions to the needy, who's consistently ranked one of the top companies to work for, who is held up as a model of the way to do business. Show me that company, and I'll show you a business who's had to bribe their way into countries like Indonesia – a business that has undoubtedly conducted some level of industrial espionage to get a leg up on the competition. A business whose flowery CEO's public persona contrasts sharply with his megalomaniacal inner demons. Those are the companies that attain the most success.

Think about it the next time you pick up a cup of coffee at your favorite café. What did it take to get that coffee into your hands? How many palms were greased? How many lives trampled? There are the footprints of twenty CEOs all over Juan Valdez's hat.

Tom Greer, all sweetness and light. I'm also available for kids' birthday parties.

Anyway, I followed Laurent, not because it was time for me to do anything, but because I was curious. Avery was feeding me Agent Baxter's whereabouts, and we were not in the same vicinity. *Lucky me*, I thought.

Laurent made three more stops that day. One for a quick bite of lunch, another to the competitor of the bank he'd been at before. Avery had found out that the Frenchman was secretly playing one against the other.

His last stop was at his favorite nail parlor. Laurent not

only got a manicure and a pedicure, but he finished up with a happy ending in the second story parlor.

I could have predicted every move. He'd made the exact same stops on his previous five trips to Jakarta. Laurent was a creature of habit, confident in his own abilities and his own personal security.

Like we'd done in Beijing, and Tokyo before that, Avery kept an eye on Laurent's movements. I ducked and hustled around the periphery, occasionally getting a view of the Frenchman as he moved farther and farther away from the city's core. For his own safety, he should have taken a cab, or even jumped on a bus. Change things up. But, again, he was a creature of habit. And he was a walker, just like me.

But then something odd happened. Just barely perceptible at first. Like a huge ocean liner gradually changing course, I felt my path turn. When I asked Avery, she said Laurent was still heading in the same general direction. No need to be alarmed.

"Where's Baxter?" I asked.

"Ten miles away, still," Avery said. She sounded bored.

I caught another glimpse of Laurent. Was it just my imagination or was he walking faster? His Dutch boy haircut bobbing as he strode comfortably down the sidewalk, he blended in with the crowds as if trying to lose a tail. It was a great strategy. Even though he was a foreigner, no one gave him a second look. He disappeared again, at least from my sight. Avery confirmed that he was still moving.

"I'm gonna let him go a couple blocks and then catch up," I said.

"Okay," Avery said around a yawn.

"Did you sleep last night?" I asked.

"Huh? Yeah. I got a little."

I'd been concerned when I'd seen Avery before leaving for Indonesia. She was too young to have those deep-set bags of black under her eyes, and yet there they were. It was the same weariness I'd seen in my sailors' contentment of a mission accomplished, but the inability to understand that they needed a break.

"I told you to get some sleep," I said.

"I know. I ignored you."

"I should have known."

"There's so much to do."

"Avery, you're not listening."

I almost told her right then and there about what had happened days before. About Baxter writing Laurent's name down after the Beijing raid. I had requested that Avery cross-check Laurent with Baxter's raid detainee, but nothing came up. No connections. No known common associates.

I kept putting it off as a coincidence. There's that word again.

Lucas Laurent. Was that a common name?

Avery's next words shook me from my pondering.

"Tom, do you see The Banker?"

"No, I told you, I was letting him go for a few minutes."

"Okay."

"What do you mean okay?"

"Well, I don't know where he went."

"What do you mean you don't know where he went?"

"He just disappeared, Tom. Jeez, I'm looking up and down the street and I can't find him."

"Back up the tape and tell me when you last saw him."

"Hang on," she said. A few seconds later, her voice returned. "Okay. He ducked into an alley about a block from where you are right now." She gave me directions.

"Keep looking. I'll see if I can catch up."

I rushed forward fast, but not too fast. No need to ping myself as a target. I found the alleyway she described. It was just wider than my shoulders. I could see that it opened up farther down. I hesitated. There was no reason to pursue Laurent right now. This was just supposed to be a casual round of surveillance.

I'm not sure what it was, but something made me put one foot in front of the other. I think it was the fact that I could almost smell him. I wanted to reach out and break every bone in his body. Sure, I was worried about the Baxter connection. And yet, maybe it was better to take care of Laurent now. Make it look like an accident or a mugging.

I crept into the alleyway, avoiding the overflowing trash heap and the puddles of fetid water. Ahead, I saw a shadow cross through the light.

I took my time now. I had a pistol in the waistband at my back. No need to pull that out yet. But I did untuck my shirt for easy access, just in case. That passing shadow put a buzz in my nerves.

Fifty feet down the alley, the space opened up, and I could see the light at the other end clearly. Maybe a hundred yards farther, between the alley opening and myself, were compact dumpsters reeking of whatever refuse local tenants used it for. My nose involuntarily crinkled. It was the smell of human waste.

Go back, Tom, the voice inside my head hissed.

Every hair on my body felt like it was standing straight up. The sixth sense tingling, like I'd been jolted by a Taser. But I was alive, and the thrill of the chase kept pulling me forward.

"Who are you?" came the question in heavily-accented English.

I spun towards the voice. There, hidden in a tiny nook behind the dumpster, was Laurent, balancing a jet-black blade on his middle finger.

"I'm sorry?" I said, trying to play it off.

"You're not British. American?" he asked.

"I don't understand."

"You've been following me. I've watched you for the last forty minutes."

"Look, I don't know what you're—"

Before I could finish my words, he'd gripped the knife and threw it straight at my chest. I barely had a chance to react. Pivoting, I tried to avoid the bite of the blade.

He barely missed my heart and the blade buried itself into my right triceps with searing pain.

I wheeled on Laurent. He had another blade out.

"Who are you?" he said. His tone was casual, unafraid. A man used to defending himself.

Now, my pistol was in hand, although the pain in my triceps made me wonder if I could shoot with my non-dominant hand. I thought about switching to my left. It was nearly as proficient, but I didn't want him to see discomfort. Instead, I reached over and pulled the blade out. I felt the blood running down my arm.

Ignore the pain for now.

Another whir. This time, I was ready. The throwing knife clanged against the alley wall, but the Frenchman had a third blade in his right hand and a fourth in the left.

DEEP THOUGHT WITH TOM GREER

Nice going, Captain. You're fucked. Now what?

OPTIONS

What would you do in that situation?

Option A: I could have shot him with my pistol. I could have taken him out right then and there. The problem? That would have alerted the neighbors.

Option B: I could have thrown the blade I pulled from my arm. But, to be honest, I was only a fair shot with my left hand when it came to throwing knives. And "fair" was being kind.

I took Option C. The Tom Greer option.

I charged, ready to deflect any blades if they flew again. They did, hitting me in the left arm and wisping off the other, slicing my right shoulder. Laurent was in the process – the calm process, I might add – of fetching more knives when I slammed into him.

He never called out. He did look me in the eyes and say those five words that overshadowed all the pain from my wounds, all the anger in my heart.

"They know you are coming," he whispered.

A momentary confusion was quickly supplanted by red rage. The black blade in my left hand went parallel and punched clean through his right temple. There was the expected spasm, and Laurent's legs kicked ineffectually against my shins.

Here comes the kicker. During the minor struggle, when I should've seen fear and death shading his complexion, his gray eyes remained locked on mine until his body gave one last shudder and I let it fall to the ground.

The body of Target Number Four collapsed into a puddle of refuse and day-old rainwater. I stood transfixed, eyes still locked with his. It felt like he was still looking at me, still giving me that silent warning.

They know you are coming.

THE CLEAN UP

I didn't tell Avery. Yeah, that was stupid, irresponsible, knuckle-headed, moronic, and downright dumb. Why do we make the choices that we do, especially in the heat of the moment?

As I stood over the body of Laurent, my mind was equal parts appeased and, once again, very aware of every detail around me. No roaming eyes, no cameras in that stinking alley.

I slipped on a pair of leather gloves that I'd never had time to put on before. I searched the body as quickly as I dared.

In my head I kept picturing Laurent's calm demeanor, the way he'd effortlessly flicked those blades at me. In a confined space, no less, and with minimal effort. It was no easy task.; throwing a blade usually takes a full arm extension. He'd somehow made his own style that was perfectly reflective of his diminutive size, a murderous dwarf with an undying engine to do me harm.

I found two more of the deadly blades inside the satchel

he'd been carrying. Other than that, nothing of value, save a few Indonesian coins. Not even a wallet.

I checked myself once, and then again. To be honest, I was a mess. I needed medical attention, but that would have to wait.

I dialed Avery's number.

She picked up on the first ring. "You find him?"

"I found him."

There was a long pause, then, "Well?"

"I took care of it".

"That's a relief. When I couldn't see you in the video feeds, I thought that maybe—"

"Listen, I'm sorry to interrupt. Can you just remind me of the way back? I need to get out of here. I got turned around."

Yes, I lied. I was hoping she wouldn't catch the hint of desperation in my voice.

I heard the shuffling of papers, like she was rustling a newspaper.

"Okay," she said, sounding put off by my curtness, "keep going down the alley. After that, take your second right..."

* * *

TWO HOURS LATER, AFTER TRACKING AND BACKTRACKING through Jakarta, scanning the crowd for familiar eyes, a telltale earring, or the same shoes, I deemed my tail clean. I stumbled into the rented apartment, the adrenaline finally leaving my body. I felt weak, parched, my wounds begging for relief.

Business first. I checked the apartment for uninvited guests. None. Always a relief when you don't have paid assassins waiting in your kitchenette.

With relief washing over me, I somehow got to the bathroom through my growing haze. The first aid kit was under the sink. I ripped off my shirt and inspected the bloody wounds. The one in my right triceps, where the blade was once buried, was the worst. Every time I flexed my arm, a gush of blood punctuated my stupidity.

After pouring Betadine on my wounds and a quick round of painful stitches, I was once again on the mend. My body had had enough. I don't remember walking to the bedroom. I don't remember collapsing on the bed. But I do remember the dreams, and they were not the glowing accolades of a job well done. They were the images of my past life, suddenly overshadowed by a coming eclipse. I should've woken myself up. I should've avoided the pain in my dream. But like the knucklehead that I am, I plunged ahead, diving headlong into the memories, already searching, for another way out.

WHERE IT GETS UGLY

Thank God I'm a quick healer. By the time our two days in Jakarta were up, I was on the mend. Back in the airport, I scanned the crowd for Agent Baxter. I found him in his customary spot, close to the gate scribbling notes furiously. I'd sent him a text the night before to cancel out on dinner, telling him I was down with food poisoning. More like down with revenge hangover.

I tossed my coffee cup into a trash bin, trying not to wince as the skin on my triceps pulled against the stitches. Baxter looked up before I got to him. I searched again for any sign of recognition that he knew what I had done. Nothing. He lifted his carry-on out of the seat next to him and pointed for me to take it.

"Good morning, Ned."

"Morning, Captain. I was going to ask you if you wanted to grab a cup of coffee, but I see you already had one."

I thought I'd been too far off for Baxter to see me. He'd been focused intently on his notebook. At least that's what I thought.

"I'm good on coffee, but I wouldn't mind grabbing a bite to eat."

"Are you feeling better?"

I rubbed my stomach. "I'm starving now, but let's just say it might be a while before I have Indonesian street food again. Oh, and it's on me. Call it repayment for canceling on dinner yesterday."

"Are you kidding? Didn't you learn anything in the Navy? If the federal government offers to pay for breakfast, you always take them up on it."

I managed to chuckle. Where the hell had the humor come from? I couldn't shake the sense that Baxter was toying with me. Maybe that was his thing, keeping people guessing. One of his many gifts. I shook it off as paranoia and followed Baxter to a restaurant he deemed appropriate for a food-poisoned stomach: McDonalds.

The flight home was uneventful. Using the same story that I'd given Baxter about the stomach bug, I let my crew do most of the heavy lifting. My co-pilot Kyle was almost ready to step up and claim his own crew. There would have to be a slightly uncomfortable conversation about resisting the urge to sleep with the female members of his future team. But I never once doubted his ability to take over. His skills as a pilot were impeccable. Eyes on the sky, hands off the crew, and you'll do just fine, son.

Baxter and I met twice on that flight in the crew cabin. He detailed a handful of ongoing investigations, peppered me with questions like he always did. I answered them truthfully, all the while checking for any hint that he was playing me. Nothing. Not a whiff of charade.

By the time we got back to the States, I was sure I was clean as polished ice in his eyes.

* * *

LAURENT SAID THEY KNEW I WAS COMING. I'D ANALYZED the way he'd said it: the subtle inflection, the way his French accent rolled out with a lisp. At some point, I realized that someone *knowing* I was coming did not mean the same as them knowing who I was. Even when I replayed the vision of his staring gray eyes in my head, there had never been that flicker of recognition in them. He'd never seen a picture of me. He couldn't have. I was nothing to him. A cipher. A random name in the phone book.

Again, my wiring could've been off. I had made the bone-headed decision. I guess I could say that I wasn't firing on all cylinders. What I needed was time to think, time to unwind and let my body mend.

I said goodbye to Baxter at the baggage claim in the Nashville airport.

"Let me know if you change your mind about the Titans game," I said. "One call and we've got two seats in the owner's suite."

"I'll think about it," Baxter said and then walked away. Guess that was a no, which sucked. Although I needed time to recuperate, I also needed to keep Baxter close. The coincidences kept piling up, and my grasp on reality was in danger of slipping.

Did Baxter know about me? Did he know about what I'd done? Had he been tracking me the whole time?

If he had, my radar needed fine-tuning. Maybe a complete overhaul. I had to come up with some other excuse to get in touch with Baxter before the next trip. Maybe I could dig up more files from the airline, deliver them personally to his suite in the Loews Hotel. He wasn't going back to D.C. in between legs this time. That was good and bad, for reasons I already mentioned.

I tried to put that out of my head as I hopped into my Uber, and we zipped off towards home.

Think, Tom, think.

* * *

TO MY SURPRISE, AVERY WAS WAITING IN THE LIVING ROOM when I got home. She'd set up shop on my coffee table, the glass top littered with empty energy drink cans and crumpled Dorito bags. And her laptop like a two-thousand-dollar paperweight on top of them.

"This is a surprise," I said.

"Hey, Tom," she said, not looking up from her computer. I was used to Avery's deep dives into cyber land.

"I'm going to take a shower and then I'll be out," I said.

"Right. Shower." She was thoroughly absorbed.

I showered carefully, not wanting to tear open my wounds and run the risk of bleeding on the carpet in front of Avery. It took longer than I would've liked.

Once I was all clean and patched up, I padded into the living room wearing a long-sleeve t-shirt and grubby jeans.

"What are you working on?" I asked walking over to the wet bar and pouring myself two fingers of Kentucky bourbon.

"Just triple-checking the notes on another file," Avery said.

"You know, I was thinking that maybe we push things back, let the playing field cool off a bit."

She finally looked up. There was something in her eyes. Relief? She replied, "I didn't want to say anything, but I was thinking that maybe we could take a little break. My parents have this thing on Sunday."

"Okay, then it's settled," I said, feeling relief myself. "You do your fancy Belle Meade thing on Sunday, and on Monday we'll get back to work."

Avery closed her laptop and started gathering up her

things. I downed half of my bourbon, relishing the cask strength liquid rolling over my tongue, warming my body.

"Do you want to stay and have a beer?" I offered.

I'd tried to get Avery to acknowledge the finer points of a good bourbon, but she was strictly a beer girl.

"I've gotta go. There are things I need to do before the party."

She avoided my gaze, but I failed to consider any reason why. What happens when two friends are so wrapped up in their own thoughts that they fail to see the warning signs?

In my experience, nothing good.

"Is there anything I can do to help? I don't know the difference between a dinner fork and a salad fork, but—"

"No, we're good," she said. "Thanks. I mean, I just... I gotta go." She looked at the garbage on the coffee table as she scooped up her bag. "Sorry. I didn't mean to trash your place."

Her eyes darted around. They had a hollow look.

"When was the last time you got a decent night's rest?" I asked.

She let out a barely audible sigh. "I've been busy."

"Yeah, you said that before." I reached out a hand and touched her shoulder. Did I feel her shiver? "I'm serious this time. Go home. Get some sleep. Hell, you can crash here if you want to."

"No, I'm fine. Like I said, I'm sorry I trashed your place."

"I told you, you can come anytime you want," I said.

"Well, sorry, but I've gotta go."

I didn't ask any more questions. Why didn't I demand that she stay? Why didn't I just make sure she got home?

Call me out. Go ahead, I can take it. I was irresponsible. I was hyper-focused on what was happening to me. I failed to open my eyes.

Hindsight's a bitch.

* * *

I WAS DEEP INTO MY THIRD BOURBON WHEN THE PHONE rang. I thought about letting it go to voicemail. I was watching a documentary on the Vietnam War. The war footage had finally snatched me from my worry. It was almost over, and I wanted to see the end.

Reluctantly, I moved to the other end of the couch and picked up my phone. The caller ID said, "Avery".

"I told you to get some sleep," I said as soon as I picked up.

"Tom." Wavering, as if spoken underwater. Fear spiked along every inch of my body. "Tom..." she said again. "*They're here*."

"What? Who is it Avery?"

"They tracked me, Tom. I'm so sorry. I should've told you—"

There was a crash and a scream.

"Avery!" I shouted in the phone. "Avery!"

But there was no reply.

Except for the sound of a muffled struggle, followed by the slam of a door.

"Avery?" I said quietly.

And waited an eternity.

CONTINGENCIES

Contingencies. You always plan for contingencies.

What happens if the bad guys find us?

What happens if the bad guys don't find us?

You plan for the worst and hope for the best.

But there's a funny thing about plans, something we say in the military: *plans never survive contact with the enemy*.

And so I stood there, frozen, trying to let my systematic brain click into place. Let it run through what I was supposed to do, instead of feeding the feelings bursting through my veins. Avery. They had her, and if they had her, it wasn't long before they knew who I was.

Think Tom, I ordered myself. Quickly, I ran to the bedroom, changed into running clothes and was out the door. Avery's apartment was a solid two miles from where I lived. I got lucky. As soon as I burst through the lobby, I saw a taxi depositing my neighbors onto the curb. I rushed in before he could get away.

"I need a ride," I said

"Sorry, have another call."

I flashed him a fifty-dollar bill. "I just need to go to West End."

There was no hesitation. "Get in," he said.

* * *

THERE WAS TRAFFIC FOR NO REASON. ANOTHER PITFALL OF the growing city. I cursed as the minutes dragged by, watching my phone, hoping Avery would call. Nothing.

"Can you please go around?" I asked the driver.

He motioned to the gridlock in front of us. "Nowhere to go."

I gritted my teeth and clamped down on the seat. I could call someone, the police, the FBI. Hell, I'd call out the National Guard if I thought it would help. In the end, my caution denied the inner request to seek aid. Better to find out what had happened firsthand. Besides, there would be questions. Questions about our relationship, questions about how I knew about Avery's disappearance.

Don't go down that hole.

I'd been part of dealing with the aftermath of kidnappings before, both overseas and on U.S. soil. I tell you this, it's never good. Unless the bad guys misplayed their hand or the authorities caught a lucky break, there wasn't much you could do except wait and watch. And I wasn't bred for waiting.

The taxi let me out three blocks from Avery's apartment. I handed over the fifty-dollar bill without saying a word. I was out and running before he could say thank you. Vander-bilt students didn't even give me a second glance as I ran by.

I glanced at my watch. It had been 14 minutes since Avery's call. Too long. *Too long dammit*. I was a block from Avery's place. I realized I'd been running a sub-six-minute pace.

Slow down, Tom. Give yourself a chance.

My eyes scanned the streets, my radar highly attuned to the environment around me.

And then, there it was ahead of me, Avery's building. There were no wailing sirens or murmuring crowds. Just what I was afraid of.

I had to put myself in the bad guys' shoes. Going out the front would have been too big of a risk. I made a beeline for the back. Hopefully, they didn't know who I was yet, just another middle-aged guy out for a run.

Still, nothing. No misplaced vans. No out-of-place thugs.

I ran to the corner, fully intending to keep going and make a pass or two just in case. But then I saw it, smashed but completely recognizable: a broken Apple watch with a Hello Kitty band. I'd given it to Avery for her last birthday.

That sent me over the edge.

Authorities and thugs be damned. Screw the danger.

I rushed to the backdoor and dialed in Avery's code. The whoosh of air conditioning greeted me as I stepped inside. I heard murmuring from down the hallway, coeds probably discussing a biology final or the way a marketing professor had screwed them on a midterm.

I cautiously took the stairs to the fourth floor, ready to grab the silenced pistol in my back waistband at any moment, or the Kershaw blade clipped to my front waistband.

The fourth floor was deserted. The lingering smell of Ramen noodle soup escorted me along.

No thugs in the passageway. No sounds.

Avery's door was the last one on the left. I tried to settle my breathing, but my heart was thudding, pushing me closer. The apartment door was ajar, just another college student leaving it open for a friend. Only I knew the truth.

If she's dead, I thought. *I'll slaughter every goddamned last one of you, today. I swear to God, I'll hang every last one of you bastards with nooses made of party streamers.*

Hinges creaked as I pushed inside. I eased the door shut behind me and locked it, pulling the pistol from my waistband. Avery's apartment was the largest in the building. Two bedrooms and a sprawling common area. She lived alone, setting up shop in the second bedroom with her array of computer gear. I wanted to go straight there to see what else they had taken.

The overturned chair and dislodged coffee table in the living room warned me to use caution. I checked the closet and the half bath. I peeked behind the kitchen counter. All clear.

On to the master bedroom. Full bath. Walk-in closet. Under the bed. Nothing. No signs of struggle. Only an unmade bed. A disgusting calm came over me. She wasn't dead. They took her. She's the bait. I'm the fish. God knows what was happening to her.

I stepped into the office. A normally tidy workspace was a combination of broken monitors, overturned trash cans and splayed file folders. Avery's familiar laptop was gone. The whirl of the fan on one of her desktop units was still going, but when I tried to get inside, it didn't work.

That's when I remembered the video surveillance system. I'd insisted on the installation. I had an almost identical one in my house. Avery said it was creepy, that I was always going overboard in my precautions. She didn't want cameras in her apartment. But I told her that if she wanted in, if she wanted to play the part of spy and assassin handler, that we had to be careful. It looked like we weren't careful enough.

The surveillance monitor was hidden behind a false wall in the office closet. It took a couple of taps on the wall to get the latch to pop out. When I got the space open, warm air from the computer components brushed against my face.

I tapped the mouse and the screen came to life. A grid of four video screens popped up to show me a live feed of

Avery's kitchen, living space, master bedroom and, finally, where I was in the office.

I went to the archived recordings and pulled up the files with recent activity. I watched helplessly as three men entered Avery's front door. They took the same path as I had, clearing as they went.

Three men against one college student equaled overkill. Maybe they hadn't known who they were dealing with. Maybe they were expecting me to be there with her.

My heart pounded as I watched them skulk into Avery's bedroom first and then went for the closed office door. At the same time, I watched the feed from the very room I was standing. Avery was on the phone, pacing back and forth. That must have been when she was talking to me. She kept glancing at the computer screen, she was watching the men on the other side of the door, who were pounding on the door now.

I couldn't hear the crash, but it replayed in my head. Two men burst through the door, fanning around the desk in the center of the room. Avery held her hands up, the phone slipping to the ground.

There was a brief struggle, but Avery was no match. One man had her pinned while another extracted something from his pocket. I zoomed in and I could just make out the shape of a syringe. He plunged the needle tip into Avery's neck and, mere seconds later, her body went slack. My gorge rose at the sight.

The third man tossed a black package into the room. He was watching the front door. The two men went to work quickly unrolling the package. It was a large duffle, big enough to fit a body.

I scanned the screen for any signs of life. Avery wasn't moving.

They couldn't have killed her, right? No way.

Was I just being hopelessly optimistic? *Oh God, not again*, I told myself as they stuffed her limp body into the black bag. *I'll swear it... I'll string you up and gut you like salmon...*

The burlier of the two men picked the bag up with two handles, tested the weight, and then eased the shoulder strap across his body. Smooth, like he'd done it a hundred times before.

He left the apartment first while thug number two searched the office. He opened drawers, broke computer screens. He didn't damage the laptop on the desk, casually depositing it into the backpack he was wearing. He peeked in the very closet I was standing in. Oh, it was a thorough search.

I stared, trying to glean some clue as to who the men were when bad guy number three, the one still in the living room, happened to glance in the direction of the video camera hidden inside the recessed can light.

I paused, then rewound the playback. There he was, clear as day. I recognized him from my list: Target Number Five, possibly the most dangerous man on the list, at least in person.

I was so consumed with what was happening on the video monitor that I barely heard a single footstep behind me.

Too late.

I felt the garrote loop over my head and tighten on my neck. My defensive reflexes kicked into overdrive. I spun around, feeling the garrote tear into my skin. At least I made it all the way around.

Now I was face to face with him.

The Executioner. Target Number Five.

THE EXECUTIONER

There was no fear in me as I locked eyes with The Executioner. There was only sick relief. His bloodshot eyes bore into mine. Hands clenched, wrapped in the white thread of a garrote. Very old school. That was The Executioner's MO. Never a gun. Almost never a blade, unless it was to silence a squealing captive. He liked to use his hands. They were a boxer's hands. Flattened knuckles. Palms rough like a rind of cheese.

My hand slapped down on his, prying him off a millimeter at a time. His eyes narrowed, sweat beading on his acned forehead, a strand of slicked back hair slipping out of place. I had a good six inches on him, but his strength more than matched mine. This was his job.

But this was my life. My life had to go on. I had to railroad through him.

With a great heave from my legs, I pushed him out of the closet, into the office. There was no stumbling, just the earth-shattering choreography of two titans locked in combat. If he registered the shift, he didn't show it. I managed to get two fingers inside the garrote. My own knuckles pressed against my trachea. What a way to go.

He must have expected me to angle him over to the desk, because he suddenly began to push me away. So I went with it, letting my body fall straight back, and letting his hands go with the same movement. Once again, I felt the pressure of the noose, cutting into skin.

We flew backward and I slammed flat on my back. A small gush of air whooshed through my lungs. He probably thought he had me, judging by the way the soft corner of his mouth released a grimace, and started to form a smile.

He didn't see my next move coming.

In the fall, I'd spread my legs wide, and now that he was on top of me, my legs were straight up in the air for a moment. But just a brief moment. I twisted to the left, letting my hips pivot with me. My right leg swung in front of his face, and I rolled with it, pinning his arms between my thighs.

I'd like to take this moment to thank the UFC for bringing Brazilian jiu-jitsu into the common world just as I did my SEAL training.

I took The Executioner with me on the roll. I won't deny that I was playing with a little bit of luck. He'd either underestimated me, or completely overestimated his own skills. He'd gotten soft by tenderizing the flesh of helpless slaves. I was no slave.

Now I was on top of him, the back of his head pressed against the floor as I, quite literally, sat on his face. My hands once again clamped over his, prying his viselike grip loose. I felt the relief immediately.

I felt a shiver of panic race through him. He could either hold onto the garrote and die or square off with his target again.

He chose Option B, letting go of the nylon cord. He bit

the meaty part of the back of my thigh, but I was beyond feeling the pain. He tried to pull the same move I did, but he was nowhere near as flexible and his legs flayed harmlessly to my sides.

For the briefest instant, I wanted to talk to him. I wanted to ask him why. But he was an animal. With the hardships he'd undoubtedly seen, he was a man bred into a beast who was only capable of doing its master's bidding.

What do you do with a rabid dog?

I slipped off him, hearing his exhale of relief. He got one breath. I heard him suck it in as I hopped to my feet, our heads pointed in opposite directions. I bent over and bear-hugged him around the waist. With a mighty heave of my legs, I jumped with our combined weight, and we were airborne. This was no Brazilian jiu-jitsu move. In moments of bitter struggle, I often marvel how comedy could so casually insert itself into a life or death drama.

As I wrapped my legs around his upper torso with The Executioner's head pointing straight at the ground, I channeled the inner Hulk Hogan of my youth. The pile driver, made famous by the wrestlers of the World Wrestling Federation.

But this was no act. No Saturday morning script. This was my life.

He tried to put his hands down. He tried to brace for impact, but it was no use. He couldn't feel the pain pulsing through my veins. But I could, and I savored every ounce of it like honey. I channeled it. His head rammed the floor, all 200-plus pounds of me as its driving force. Gravity, baby. It does the most wondrous of things.

I felt the neck snap and the body go limp, but I continued the momentum, holding him close, legs flopping against my ears, until he settled. I threw his body away like it was diseased.

Breathe.

I searched him and found a cellphone in his pocket. That could come in handy. There was nothing else, save the garrote now lying partially under his lolling head. I hadn't planned on it, but five of seven were down, gone, wiped from the earth.

Two more to go.

* * *

But that wasn't my immediate concern.

Avery? Where was she? Where had they taken her? Maybe the cellphone in my hand would help.

I heard the screams of sirens close by. Were they coming for me? No time to find out.

I took one last look at my latest victim, his tongue hanging from his mouth. I rushed out of the apartment. Thankfully, no one was in the hallway. Maybe someone down-stairs had heard the commotion and called the cops. Maybe.

I was clear of the hallway and all the way to the stairwell entrance when my cellphone buzzed. Thinking it might be Avery, or her captors, I pulled it out expectantly.

Great. I almost ignored the call. It was my ex-wife. The stairwell was empty, so I answered and I bounded down the stairs.

"Hey, Laura," I said, trying to sound nonchalant.

"Tom?"

I tried not to sound impatient. "I'm kind of busy right now."

"The nursing home called," she said.

That got my attention. *Great*. "Why did they call you?"

"They said they tried to contact you, but that you didn't answer."

I pulled the phone from my ear and looked back to my call log. There'd been three missed calls. *Hi, you've reached*

Tom. Sorry, I can't answer the phone right now, I am busy fighting for my life.

"I'm sorry, Laura. I didn't even know you were on the list."

"I didn't either," she said. "Your dad added me to the emergency contact list, that's what they said."

My gruff, unforgiving father had always loved Laura. He never even joked with me, but Laura was like the daughter he never had. I'd often catch them trading jokes in the kitchen, my father laughing uproariously at something that Laura had said. He never did that with me.

"Thanks for calling, Laura, I..."

"Is everything okay, Tom? You sound ..."

"No, I'm fine. I'm just in a rush. I'll call when I get everything settled."

"The nursing home said your dad was pretty upset. Do you want me to come down? I don't mind."

"No," I said. "I can handle it."

"Okay."

My tone had done it. She knew when to quit. She'd seen my anger. She was better at controlling emotions than I was. But in that second, I didn't care.

I burst outside, phone still connected to my ear.

"Tom, we should talk some time," she said.

"Yeah, sure."

"But I really think we should—"

I knew what was coming, so I cut her off. "I'm fine. You're fine. Can't we leave it at that?"

"But that's the thing, Tom, I don't know if—"

"I said I have to go. Thanks for the heads-up."

I hung up before she could continue. I didn't have time for this shit.

Take a second, Tom.

I had my guesses of where they could have taken Avery.

This had to be orchestrated by Targets Six and Seven, and I still had access to all of Avery's files. Every location. Every recorded video feed of every single one of our targets. I would track them down. I would find her.

But what happened next killed my budding plans. The other phone rang. The one I'd taken from the dead guy in Avery's apartment.

I stared down at it.

Unknown Caller.

Hell, I answered it.

HOSTAGE NEGOTIATION

"Hello," I answered, barely settling my words from the exertion.

"Who is this?" the voice said on the other end.

"You know who it is," I answered.

There was a pause and then a low chuckle. "Ah, Mr. Greer." Then a playful mock-German accent. "Zo, vee finally meet!"

I didn't have to ask how he knew my name. It had to be through Avery. It had been, what, maybe half an hour? And they'd already broken her.

"What have you done with—"

"Now, Mr. Greer," Number Six interrupted. I knew that voice well. I'd listened to hours of tape with him droning on and on to his subordinates. He was a long-winded one. "It seems as though I have something you need, and you have something that I desire."

"I don't have anything—"

Again, he cut me off. "Tut tut, Mr. Greer. If you wish to see your young friend released *relatively* unharmed, you will do as I say."

"And what do you want?"

A low chuckle. "We want *you*, Mr. Greer. My friends are quite, how shall I put it, *intrigued* by your skills. Taking down one of our team members is no small feat, but to kill five of our men without detection? Such extraordinary talent. We appreciate talent when we find it, Mr. Greer. And so I applaud you. Perhaps there's a way we can—"

"No," I said, knowing where the conversation was going. I'd heard this man utter the same platitudes with others, former enemies that he'd somehow convinced, usually through coercion or simple bribery, to flip sides. But before I uttered another word, those distant conversations gave me an idea.

"If we do it, we do it my way," I said.

"Do what, Mr. Greer?"

"I only care that my friend is safe. You let her go now and I'll do anything you want."

"Now that wasn't so hard, was it?" he purred. "But, pardon me, I don't trust you. I don't know your whole plan, but the two men escorting Miss Avery say it's not long before we dissect her and find out the truth. I think I'll wait until after that's done to bargain with you. Her screams will be like Mozart, Mr. Greer."

"That won't stop the others," I blurted.

"Others," he said with a chuckle.

"Yeah, others. Avery doesn't know about them. It was my back-up plan in case something happened to me or her."

"I don't know if I believe you, Mr. Greer. Miss Avery was more than happy to admit that it was just the two of you. She's got quite the voice. A little bit of pain and—"

"Knock it off," I said. "I told you, she doesn't know about the others in the network."

"Then one of you is lying. I can't pry the truth out of you, but I can easily—"

"Don't you fucking touch her!"

"My, my. Such language. Touchy subject, is it? Maybe you should have thought of that before involving her in this pointless vendetta of yours. Isn't that one of the codes of you heroes? Never involve innocents? Sickening. Well, she's involved now, Mr. Greer. There's no turning back."

"I swear, if you—"

He tsked at me over the phone. "There's a flight tomorrow, Nashville to Salt Lake City. All the arrangements have been made. Check in at the Southwest terminal. You will receive further instructions upon landing in Salt Lake City. Oh, and Mr. Greer, one more thing..."

I heard a series of clicks and then someone else's voice said, "Go ahead."

"Tom, oh Tom, help me! Help me!" Avery screamed, and the line went dead before I could tell her I was coming.

THE ADMIRAL

In that moment, I would have done anything to end Avery's pain. It was probably a good thing that I couldn't call the guy back. Decisions made in such an emotional state are, ill-advised.

It had been long a part of my DNA to detach myself from a given situation. Part of it was the way I was raised, but more of it was the way I'd been trained. A Navy SEAL can't lose his cool. An airline pilot in a freak thunderstorm can't get the jitters.

Then again, they always tell you that your training flies out the window when the safety of a loved one is concerned. That's why having a family member in your military unit is still mostly considered taboo. Ask the Sullivan family and the five brothers who lost their lives together during WWII.

So yeah, it was a good thing I couldn't call back. It gave me time to think. It gave me time to breathe.

Breathe, Tom. In and out.

I focused on my breaths.

In and out.

I put myself through an abbreviated version of my medi-tation routine.

In. Out.

Focus on the breaths. Push the other thoughts aside.

In. Out.

Images of Avery being strangled. Electrocuted... burned with acid...

In. Out.

Avery screaming in my head.

In. Out.

Avery's cold body lying on a metal gurney.

My eyes smacked open.

No, I said to the world. *Think, Tom*. Contingencies.

I had friends I could call. Tough warriors who would drop everything to come to my aid. I'd done it for them. They'd run to the fury without a single question.

No. No need to put them in harm's way. They'd given enough.

The studious face of Agent Baxter popped into my head as I opened the Uber app on my phone. Maybe I could alert Baxter. He could pull some strings. Then again, involving him meant questions. It wasn't that I necessarily cared about the outcome for me, but what would a full-blown FBI investiga-tion do to Avery's life?

Yeah, I know what you're thinking. Who cares about the consequences when you're dangling by your ankles over a crocodile pit?

Sue me. I thought about such things.

No, I wouldn't be calling the FBI, but there was one person I had to see. The one person who would understand.

A navy blue Nissan Armada that would take me there pulled up to the curb 10 minutes later, and the middle-aged woman driving waved to me with a smile. I climbed in the

back and did my best to keep up a normal conversation until
we arrived.

* * *

"How is he today?" I asked the nurse on duty.

"We tried to call you, Mr. Greer."

"I know. My wife... I mean my ex-wife, told me."

The nurse was new. She didn't know my story.

"Well, your *ex*-wife was very nice. She offered to
come down."

"No, that won't be necessary." Then I paused and said,
"I'm going out of town for a few days. If there is an emergency, forget what I just said. Call my ex-wife. She'll know
what to do."

The nurse dutifully made a note in my father's file.

"Mr. Greer, we had to restrain your father again."

"I understand."

The nurse looked like she wanted to say more.

"What is it?" I asked.

"It's just, they told me not to say anything, but..."

"What happened?" I asked, trying to sound calm, but the
way her eyes were darting around, it wasn't putting me
at ease.

"He just kept saying the same thing over and over. I don't
think he was going to hurt anybody or hurt himself, but..."

"They told you it was safer to have him restrained," I
finished for her.

She nodded.

"Have you ever seen anything like that before?" I asked.

"Just in training videos. I only started last week."

Welcome to reality, I thought, but didn't say it out loud.

"He doesn't know what he's saying. That's the problem
with his disease."

"But it was just the way he was saying it. He was so adamant. I swear he was completely lucid when I talked to him. Has his diagnosis ever been..."

"That's natural," I said. "It comes and goes."

"Yeah, but Mr. Greer, I—"

Just then, Phyllis, the nurse manager walked into the room and the young nurse shut her mouth.

"Oh, hello, Mr. Greer, how are you today?" the woman said. I didn't particularly like her. She reminded me of strap hangers in the military. People who coasted along and milked their career for everything it was worth. They never did anything too wrong to get fired. And when they were promoted, they got their very own clipboard. I had observed on more than one occasion how this particular nurse manager kissed just the right asses to keep her job.

"I'm fine, thank you, Phyllis." I turned back to the young nurse. "Why don't you tell me the rest on the way to my dad's room?"

"Oh, I can take you," said Phyllis, throwing a satisfied look at her young charge.

"No, that's okay." I looked down at the girl's name tag. "Martha and I were just getting acquainted. I'm sure you have plenty to do."

Phyllis gave an internal harrumph, but pasted on a fake smile. "Okay, but don't be long, Martha. There are bedpans to be cleaned after all."

Yep, a dime a dozen.

Martha followed me from around the counter. Phyllis was already settling into a desk chair like sitting was her job. Once we were out of earshot, I asked the young nurse, "What was my father saying?"

"You promise you won't tell anyone?"

"Like who? Phyllis? Don't worry, I'm on your side, not hers."

"Okay." She gnawed her bottom lip for a moment. "He was screaming. At first, I didn't understand what he was saying. I heard him from the other end of the hall. I came running. I didn't want him to hurt himself. I thought that maybe he was fighting with someone, but when I got to his room he was just staring out the window yelling."

"What was he saying?"

She shook her head like she didn't want to go there. "It's like he was replaying a scene in his head. I really thought he was watching someone outside."

"What did he say, Martha?"

She was slowing down now that we were getting closer to my father's room. "I don't remember everything, but..."

"Just tell me what you remember."

Martha stopped in the middle of the hall and looked up at me. Her eyes were rimmed with tears. "He said it was *his fault*. It took me a minute to realize he was screaming at God. He kept telling God to take him, that he didn't deserve to live." She was suppressing a sob.

"Hey, it's okay," I said.

She produced a Kleenex from her pocket and was dabbing her eyes.

"Martha, I'll take care of it, okay?"

She nodded and walked away.

Dad had experienced screaming episodes before, but this was a new one. Maybe it was a sign of what was to come. The final cracking up. His brain giving in. Well, at least I'd get a chance to say goodbye.

When I entered the room, I cringed when I saw that he was strapped to the bed by his arms and legs. It was like seeing a once-mighty lion cuffed to a metal chain in a dingy corner of a decrepit zoo in a long-forgotten city. He was staring straight ahead. I wondered, not for the first time, what he saw through those eyes.

"Hey, Dad," I said, placing a hand on his arm.

His head turned. "Tommy?"

"Yeah, Dad, it's me."

"Back from Iraq, or is it Afghanistan this time? I can't... for some reason I can't remember."

"Yeah, Dad, I'm back," I said, playing along. It was best just to go with whatever timeline his mind was currently latched onto.

"What do they have me in for this time?" he asked, glancing at his restraints.

"You don't remember?"

I don't know why I said it. It was cruel and I saw his face twist, his mind searching.

"Was I drinking again?"

"No, Dad, you weren't drinking." He hadn't had a drop in twenty years. Self-imposed, cold turkey, just The Admiral's style.

"Molesting the nurses?"

"Dad, I just came to tell you something."

"You're going away again. It's okay, give it to me. That's the life we've chosen."

God, it was like he was all better again. Tough as nails and stoic to a fault.

I remember when my wife had tried to get me and my dad to hug before I left the first time for Afghanistan. It had been an awkward affair. Admiral Greer was not a hugger.

Then Avery's words from the cemetery came again. "What if...?"

They'd done scans and tests. Nothing. Healthy as far as the computers could tell.

The doctors lumped it in as dementia with a sprinkle of Alzheimer's on the side. It wasn't the first time I'd been disappointed by the half-answers of the medical establishment.

I stared down at The Admiral, wanting him to break his bonds and come with me. I needed him now more than I ever had.

I was about to say something else, some loving gesture that he would never remember, a final goodbye even. But then, I saw his features cloud over, the confusion returned.

"Tommy, did you just get here?" He looked down at his hands again. "Why am I tied down?"

"Dad, it's okay," I reached down and undid the strap on his right wrist.

He immediately flexed his hand and even patted his hip like he was looking for a side arm. I grabbed his hand and held it.

"Dad, I have to tell you something."

"Son, help me out of this bed. I need to... to..."

"No, just lay there and listen."

His eyes had cleared again and he nodded. He was fully there, so I told him. I told him everything. I told him what I'd done and what I still needed to do. I told it the way he'd told me after I earned my trident: to the point, unemotional, completely my father's son.

When I was finished, I bent over, hugged him, and kissed him on the forehead.

"I love you, Dad. I'll see you soon."

"The cemetery dirt's cold, son," he said with a voice like gauze.

His eyes followed me as I left the room. I couldn't help but mourn the fact that he couldn't come with me. His once brilliant mind crippled by an old man's disease. What a waste.

"Goodbye, Dad," I said quietly. "I'll meet you on the other side."

SALT LAKE CITY TO SEOUL

The next day, I did as I was instructed. Reservations were waiting to take me from Nashville to Salt Lake City. The first leg was uneventful and as I walked through the Salt Lake City airport, I ran through my options for the hundredth time. I'd committed what I could about the rest of my targets to memory, and there was no further communication from Number Six, until now.

"Thomas Greer. Thomas Greer, please report to Gate B12." The official statement came over the intercom.

I hurried to B12, my senses roving as I went, taking apart the crowd, feeling it out for inherent danger. All I saw were typical harried travelers.

I got to Gate B12 and the destination sign read, "Seoul, Korea." A businessman in a rumpled suit hurried past me and handed his boarding pass to the gate agent. I waited until he'd fumbled through, then approached the agent.

"Excuse me, ma'am. You paged me?"

"Mr. Greer?"

"That's me."

The agent nodded, closed the jet bridge door, and hurried

over to the desk. "You almost missed boarding," she said, logging into her computer.

Best not to ask any questions, I thought to myself. If Number Six wanted me on this flight, I was on this flight.

Thirty seconds later, the agent handed me a boarding pass.

"Here you go, Mr. Greer."

"Were there any further instructions?" I asked.

"I'm sorry?"

"My friend, the one who scheduled my flights, he was supposed to send me instructions."

She looked back down at the screen. "No, sir. One Business Elite reservation was all I got."

"Okay, thanks. Do I have time to run to the bathroom?"

She looked up at the digital clock. "I'm afraid not."

Three minutes later, I was settled into my elite class seat. It was one of the newest 777 models. Plush and spacious, you felt like you were in your own private cabin as long as you were sitting down. I did a quick, casual glance around the cabin, trying to pinpoint any babysitters that might be along for the ride, but no one stood out. The crew was courteous and efficient, dare I say almost as good as my own.

Ten minutes later, we were taxiing down the runway. I closed my mind and tried to imagine what would happen next.

The problem with most imaginations is that they can never quite pinpoint the horror of reality.

* * *

I THINK I HAD JUST FALLEN ASLEEP WHEN WE TOUCHED down in Seoul. I was groggy and temporarily out of place. I'd been dreaming about my old life. Perfect, vanilla, resplendent with a white picket fence. A flight attendant came by and offered me a hot towel. I took it gratefully, wiped my face and arms and handed it back to her. She left and was soon replaced by her coworker, who sidled up with a smile.

"Mr. Greer?"

"Yes?"

She handed over an envelope. "I hope you had a nice flight," she said and walked away.

I examined the envelope. It had my name on the front: *Thomas Greer, Jr.* I slid it open carefully. There was another envelope inside, and written on it were simple instructions:

You'll be met at baggage claim.

Efficient. Had that note gotten into the hands of the flight crew before takeoff or during flight from one of the passengers? I thought about asking the flight attendant, but then I realized there was no need to embroil them in my business. It was obvious my enemy had a tidy way of cleaning up loose ends.

I gathered up my belongings and followed the rest of the passengers off the plane and into the airport.

I was still holding the second envelope when I closed the stall in the first restroom I came to. I didn't want to open it, but I knew I had to. I ripped open the seal, already knowing what I would find.

Like ripping off a Band-Aid, I snatched the photo out of its compartment. It was a grainy photo of Avery stripped down to her bra and panties and tied to a chair. Her eyes were wide with fear. I thought I detected bruises on the left side of her face, but I couldn't tell from the shadows.

I tore up the photo and the envelope and flushed them down the toilet.

They were going to pay. Even if it took me until my very last breath, those bastards were going to pay.

SCHULTZ

A young Korean boy of no more than twelve was waiting in the baggage claim with a sign that read, "Thomas Greer, Jr."

How efficient.

He didn't speak, but waved me to the exit. We walked to the very last spot, where a boxy Rolls-Royce was waiting. Two policemen were standing at the curb, no doubt keeping the common folk from touching the luxury automobile.

The boy opened the back door. In I went, sliding onto the plush leather, taking in the view.

And there he was: Target Number Six. Marco Schultz. Alabaster skin, a modern day dandy, the look of someone who bathed in rose petals daily. His delicate features and snakelike eyes stood out in deep contrast to one another.

"Mr. Greer," he said with oil in his voice, "how nice of you to come."

"As if I had a choice. Where's Avery?"

The Rolls started moving, although I could barely feel a bump. It rode low and heavy, like an armored carrier that had been given the sweet touch of German engineering. German, just like the man sitting in front of me. I knew little of his background, but much of his current business dealings.

"We'll get to our young friend in due time."

I didn't like the way he said *our* like he'd already taken possession of her. Schultz had a certain proclivity for young boys and girls, more like the Korean boy who'd fetched me from baggage claim, and hopefully less like someone of Avery's age. I tried not to squirm in my seat.

"I wanted to have a word with you before we visit your friend."

"What about?" I asked, trying to still the bile in the back of my throat.

"Your background, it's... *intriguing*."

"How so?"

"You were a Navy SEAL, decorated in combat numerous times. And yet you left your career when many said you could've picked up a star, just like your father."

I didn't have time to think about how he'd come by that information.

"And now, you're an airline pilot. Tell me. How does one make such a career move?"

I shrugged and crossed one leg over the other.

"I signed my discharge papers, and then I went back to school to upgrade my pilot's license."

"And somehow you were pulled back into, how should I put it, this special business. You never can shake it, can you, Mr. Greer? Once you get a taste of the violence. I wonder. Do you like the fear in their eyes, or the scent of blood? Or both?" He shook his head with a grin. "Never mind, don't answer that question. We'll get to it in time. Each of us has our own tastes." He ran a finger over his lips, I could see the gloss from his latest manicure. "While your background is interesting to me and to my associates, the broader question still remains: What made us cross paths?"

I knew the question was coming, and I'd been thinking about my answer since talking to him on the phone outside Avery's building. There was no way I could tell him the truth. I still didn't know what Avery told him. She could've told him everything, at least what she knew.

In that case, this conversation was just a game. A game that Herr Schultz played very well. All I saw in his eyes was curiosity, like he just met the most interesting man on the planet. He was truly engaged.

I went with a sprinkle of truth and a dash of fiction.

"Flying is my cover. It gets me wherever I need to go. What you've alluded to is my, how should I put it, full time gig now."

"You still haven't answered my question. How did we cross paths, Mr. Greer?"

I shrugged, nonchalantly. "A mistake."

"What sort of mistake?"

"My current employer had a task that needed to be done. But I am a businessman, Mr. Schultz. It doesn't matter who I work for. It's a free market, and I am a free agent. Pay me more and let go of my friend, and I'm happy to discuss how I can sever ties with my current employer. Obviously, he doesn't have your cunning."

Schultz mulled that over for a moment. "And why should I believe you, Mr. Greer? You've killed five of my men. Good, reliable, hardworking men. It will take more than a fortnight to replace them."

"I didn't say you should believe me," I said. "I said I'm open for bidding."

I just needed to keep him on the hook long enough, long enough to get close to Avery, and then.... Well, I didn't really have a plan after that. They could shoot me in the back of the head as soon as I left the car. Avery might already be dead. But I had to hope that Schultz's curiosity wasn't just an act.

He wanted something. Maybe it was me. Maybe it was what I knew. Maybe it was just to find out the real answer.

Well, he'd have to dig deep for that one.

As if reading my thoughts, Schultz's hand slid into a pocket and came out holding a Walther PPK pistol.

How very James Bond, I thought.

"I think you're lying to me, Mr. Greer. Our young friend is moments away from telling us the truth. Why don't you make it easier for her and tell us first? All I have to do is make a phone call and her pain stops. I've had no less than three of my men, men whose morals have... how should I say, slipped over the years, who have volunteered to enjoy some personal time with Avery."

I sat stock still, trying not to let my emotions show. *God, don't let him know what I'm thinking.*

"Look, the girl works for me. Nothing more. There's no emotional attachment. She's not my daughter, not my girl-friend. If you harm her, that just hurts my business. You know I'm telling the truth. If the girl had any worth as emotional leverage, you wouldn't need that gun."

He smiled. "It's not easy replacing talent, is it, Mr. Greer?" I shook my head. Two business owners, seemingly in agreement.

"Do you know," he continued, "I have to hire ten to get one good man? Oh, but when I find a true gem, someone worthy of respect and admiration, I keep him at all costs. So I understand your concern." The Rolls came to a stop and Schultz looked out the window. "Ah, here we are."

We'd pulled into a lower level garage under a high-rise office building. The light from outside was snuffed out as the garage door closed behind us.

"Now, if you will excuse me, Mr. Greer, I have important matters to attend to." The back door opened and he said, "I hope your stay with us is a comfortable one."

Two sets of strong arms reached in and yanked me out. I felt a hard elbow smack into my temple. It knocked me sideways, but it wasn't the blurred vision or the hood they put over my head that worried me.

It was the screams of pain echoing in the shadows. The shrieks broadcasting pure agony. The screams haunted me as I felt a second blow to my head, and my world faded to black.

A BUZZ IN THE AIR

I came to with a splash. They'd dumped a bucket of ammonia on me. My hands involuntarily went to cover my face but they wouldn't move.

I looked down through blurred vision, shaking my head and spitting. I saw I was strapped to a chair. I couldn't see past the glaring light, but I noticed my own body was stripped down to my underwear, electrodes placed in identical spots on each thigh, each forearm. I squinted at the wires dangling from the sides of my head.

So much for playing the recruitment angle. Maybe Avery had finally cracked. Now that they had me in custody, a full court press was inevitable. What little consolation I could salvage from the situation was that Avery didn't know the whole truth, not that it helped either of us at that moment.

I shook my head, clearing the final cobwebs of unconsciousness. I felt groggy, like they'd pumped me with drugs. All sense of time was gone. It could have been noon or midnight. No idea. Suddenly, the blazing light strobed, *flash flash flash*, and then turned off. Again, *flash flash flash* and then off, like they were trying to reprogram my brain, or maybe just wake me up. I wanted to yell and tell them to cut it out. Instead, I stared straight ahead into the light, daring them to keep it up.

The light dimmed and I saw shadows pass through the spotlight.

"You're awake," a voice said. It was Schultz. "How are you feeling?"

"Peachy."

"I told them to give you a little bit of Toradol for the headache. They slipped it in with the sedative. You didn't strike me as someone who would stay unconscious for long without help." He chuckled. "You're the second SEAL we've had the pleasure of hosting. The first? Well, let's just say he wasn't as well-mannered as you. Always cursing. So distasteful. You're an officer and a gentleman?"

I didn't bother to answer.

"I must look into this. I confess I don't have a good grasp of military custom. I am, however, a voracious reader of historical text. We can glean such insight, so many lessons from our past. I admit to being a bit biased. I gravitate towards my own people, the Germans. Like Adolf Hitler, as an example. Oh, don't get squeamish, Mr. Greer. Hitler was a bit sloppy in his methods, but his intentions were as sound as any great leader's. He was a nobody, thrown in jail. 99.99 percent of the rest of humanity would have taken it. They would have gone home and lived the peasant lifestyle, or maybe taken a job as a simple clerk. But not our dear Führer. Look at how he galvanized a nation. Yes, his techniques were crude, but, well, I'm not so sure I believe all that stuff about the supposed death camps anyway."

"What's your point?" I asked.

"Now, Mr. Greer, don't be rude. I thought that maybe we could have a nice chat."

"Why don't you strip down to your skivvies and then we'll have a nice chat."

He chuckled. "I'm sorry, but you're not quite my type." He moved closer to me now. "I must say, you are quite the specimen for your age." He traced a finger from my shoulder along my collarbone. "At another time. At another time," he mulled aloud. He then put the finger in his mouth, as if testing cake icing. After snapping his tongue, he said, "Now, what are we to do with you, Mr. Greer? You've interrupted business. You've broken part of our pipeline."

"Tough."

"There's that rudeness again. Maybe I was wrong about you. What of your friend, young Avery? Was she wrong about you as well? She says so many kind things of you. You would almost believe that she was in love with you." He shuddered cartoonishly. "Ah, well."

He turned back to the light and made a 'turn it down' gesture to whomever was controlling. The light dimmed some more and he turned back to me, extracting a thin remote from his pocket as he did so.

"This, Mr. Greer, is something I was hoping we wouldn't have to use." He pressed a button and I felt my thighs tighten involuntarily. It wasn't uncomfortable. More like something I'd felt during the rehabilitation of my knee.

He pressed the button again and my leg slackened.

"That was the lowest voltage," he said. I could barely feel it. Now he clicked a couple buttons. "And this... is where most people break."

Bracing for impact was impossible. The pain hit my legs and all I saw was red. When he released the power button again, I realized I was moaning.

"You see, Mr. Greer, there is no escaping the pain. If I want you to feel it, you will, but if you tell me the truth and I believe you, we can make your death painless. A warrior's death, isn't that what you call it? A bullet to the head, or I have associates who enjoy a knife to the heart. I'll leave it to you."

He didn't warn me the next time. I assume he pressed the button because every millimeter of my body screamed as it tensed against the restraints. When he released me, I slumped in the chair, gulping in breaths.

"My colleagues believe I should soften you up. I don't think that's necessary. Do you?" Again, he didn't wait for my answer. "I'm a patient man. I'm happy to indulge your fantasy for weeks, if need be. Hold out. It doesn't really matter. If you think you've really done harm to our organization, you're wrong. It's just like your pathetic war on terror. Chop off one head and five more rise up to replace it."

He started pacing back and forth in front of me.

"No, my curiosity is more profound. I would like to know more about *you*, Mr. Greer. Tell me what your friend doesn't know. Tell me your deepest, darkest secrets. If I am appeased by your tales, I will give you the death that I promised. If not, well, we've already talked about that, haven't we? I don't like to repeat myself. Because I know not everyone is like me. My mother said I was made from a new mold. Maybe you do need a reminder." He pointed the remote straight at me and smiled, "Let's see how tough you really are, Mr. Greer. Oh, and feel free to cry out. Let it out, Mr. Greer. Pray aloud, if you like. I want to hear some enthusiasm."

Then he pressed the button, sending a current of pain through my body that must have been summoned up from the lowest pits of hell.

SENSE AND SENSELESS

The next time I awoke, my sense of taste greeted me at the pass.

Copper? Or was it iron? Bitter and metallic on my tongue. Blood, of course.

I tried to swallow, but my swollen tongue wouldn't allow it. I stifled a gag.

My body came next. Every muscle felt weak and tender as I ran through an internal diagnostic. It was like I had the most sadistic personal trainer who would keep me sore for a month. Even my eyelids hurt.

I somehow managed to crack my eyes open, the dimmed-out light adding to my discomfort and headache. I would've given almost anything for a sip of water. The human body can do miraculous things, but when deprived of certain basic needs, like water for instance, the body tends to rebel. That rebellion currently manifested itself in a cotton mouth and, as I squeezed certain muscles along my body, those fibers responded by cramping painfully, locking up tight.

Breathe, I willed myself.

Slowly, I did.

Slowly, the cramps went away and then I heard a whisper in my subconscious.

Tom. Tom, wake up.

It was Avery's voice. What did that mean? Was I going crazy now? Had Schultz fried my brain? Was I destined to a shortened life, damaged like my father?

I heard the whisper again. *Tom.*

I don't know why, but I opened my eyes, maybe just for the unreal validation that I wasn't going crazy. It took several blinks for my vision to clear. I was sitting in a chair, and there was something dark before me.

I realized that I was in a leather office chair, and the object in front of me was a conference table. There were three seats on each side, one of those intercom speaker systems in the middle of the table, and then to my surprise and horror, I saw at the other end, the source of the sound.

It was Avery. One eye was swollen shut and her right ear was caked with blood, hair stuck to it at skewed angles.

I tried to speak but my swollen tongue wouldn't let me.

"Tom," she whispered. "Can you hear me? I think they're coming."

I moved my tongue around in my mouth. I needed to speak. I didn't know how much time I had. I had definitely bit through my tongue, because it wasn't playing ball. All I needed was some water.

Some water, dammit!

I wanted to ask her if she was okay, wanted to tell her that I would get her out of this, but I never got the chance. Before I could build up enough saliva to respond, the only door in the room opened and Schultz marched in followed by five henchmen, each one

dressed impeccably. Five lackeys masquerading as corporate suits.

But the real surprise came as the last man entered the room. We locked eyes.

Agent Baxter.

I pushed forward against my restraints and slurred something incoherent.

"Please do be quiet," Schultz said, taking a seat to my left. "I told them not to gag you, but I'm more than willing to stuff a sock into your mouth. Now, for introductions. The man sitting across from me..." He went on to introduce them one by one, like prize ponies at a fair. The second, my executioner. The third was Schultz's personal legal representation.

When my captor came to Baxter, my worst fears were confirmed.

"And the man with the studious look at the far end of the table, next to our friend Avery, is an agent with your Federal Bureau of Investigations."

Baxter stared me down and merely nodded at Schultz's comments. Not a flicker of recognition. I waited for the hammer to fall.

I anticipated Schultz's next words: "He's been following you, Mr. Greer," I imagined him saying. "We know everything you've done. The mole inside the FBI sealed your fate."

But the words never came.

Baxter kept his mouth shut while Schultz droned on about the complicated situation.

"Water," I just managed to get out.

Schultz looked at me in annoyance for interrupting him. He nodded to one of his lackeys, who left the room and returned a moment later with a metal pitcher glistening in cold sweat and a glass. He poured the ice water into the glass, set the glass on the table, and looked down at me, smirking.

I wasn't going to beg, but I wasn't above leaning over to where I could tilt the glass back with cracked lips and feel the ice-cold water pass over my tongue and down my parched throat.

The others waited as I savored what victory I could out of the glass. I wasn't even a sixth of the way through when the same goon snatched the glass from my lips and retook his seat, sipping at the remains of that glorious water. You'd be amazed what a little water can do for the soul.

I looked down at Avery and gave her a reassuring nod, although it did little to change the shell shock plastered on her face.

Schultz cleared his throat. "Despite what you might think of me, Mr. Greer, I am a man of my word. When I say something will be done, it will. Go ahead and think what you want about our organization. It's based on rules and a strict hierarchy. Now, gentlemen, if you wouldn't mind, please untie Miss Avery."

Two men converged on Avery and made her panic. She squirmed in her chair, and I tried to rip myself from mine.

Strong hands were soon holding us both down and Schultz knocked lightly on the table until he had gotten our full and undivided attention.

"I think you both misunderstood me. My promise was to let our young friend go."

"Why?" I asked hoarsely, knowing it was all a charade.

Schultz turned on me with a look of annoyance, "Because I promised," he said, slapping his hand palm down on the table. "And when I make a promise—" he didn't finish his sentence. Instead, he composed himself and looked down at Avery. "Young Miss, you will be watched from today onward. We know who you are. Unlike your friend Mr. Greer, I hope you can see reason. Feel free to live your life. Go back to Tennessee, finish school, but don't try to find us. My associate from the FBI will be monitoring your activity. Do you understand?"

She stared at me, unmoving.

"I said, do you understand?"

Avery gave a timid nod.

"Good, then it's—"

"What about Tom?" Avery interrupted. "What will you do with him?"

"I made him a promise as well. Didn't I, Mr. Greer?"

I didn't answer.

"Agent Baxter," said Schultz, "if you will escort our young American to my residence, she may get cleaned up before her departure."

Baxter nodded and rose from the table. He'd mostly avoided my gaze since entering the room. Was it cowardice? Was he ashamed of the fact that he was part of this criminal undertaking?

How had we missed him? I guess you can't say we missed him, he'd been there all along. We just missed the signs.

Avery went to speak, "Tell me what —"

Baxter slapped her across the face so hard that she would have spun around 180 degrees if Baxter hadn't caught her. The men left with her.

Schultz turned to face me. He snatched a yellow handkerchief from his lapel pocket and dabbed a blot of dried blood on my arm.

"You are a mess, Mr. Greer. What shall we do with you?"

No answer was needed, we both knew what was going to happen eventually. It was the timeline between my death and right now that I steeled myself for.

"That young woman had wonderful tales to tell about you, but I must say that I got the distinct impression that there were holes in her narrative. I told my associates not to press too hard. I didn't tell her, but I will tell you that I might have use for her in the future. I've disposed no fewer than three of my supposed experts for their deficiency in tracking down your young accomplice. Perhaps she will take a role in our growing organization one day. But in order to do so, I had to allow her to think that she had won, even if it was a small victory."

He tossed the handkerchief in my lap and took in a deep breath before continuing.

"She alluded to some vendetta. Tenacious young woman. It would have been interesting to see if she'd held out for another day, maybe two." He leaned in close now. "But she didn't know the whole truth, did she, Mr. Greer? She knew the truth that you wanted her to believe. There's something darker inside you. Only something so insidious would take an honorable man and pit him against, well, myself. So what happens now is that the truth will be ripped from your very being. At the end of your time with us, you will beg not only for mercy, but also for death. And make no mistake about one thing, Mr. Greer: I will have the truth, and you will give it to me."

PAIN

As an operator, you always wonder how you'd fare in an intensive interrogation. You plan for it. You think about it. You read up on famous POWs like Senator John McCain. You try to pick up on tips and tricks. You listen to their lectures, but nothing really prepares you for the real thing.

My path through torture was probably the same as millions who had gone before me. Sleep deprivation, light deprivation, sensory overload. In my head, I called that Phase One. During Phase One, they didn't ask me a single question. It both heightened and dulled my senses. I heard every creak of my cell door, but I barely noticed when the lights went from red hot to black cold.

I held up pretty well during that time. I lost all track of minutes, hours and days. I had moments of perfect clarity and then hours of delirium. Occasionally, they would bring in bottled water and one of my guards would place it to my lips. He'd give me exactly five seconds to drink as much as I could. Water, but no food.

At some point, Phase Two began. Schultz did the questioning with the help of one of his sadistic lackeys. This particular specimen never laid a hand on me, but he did have an ingenious tool. Something so simple that even I, in my battered state, could admire its beauty, like a throwback to the first days of man.

It was a thin, wooden rod whose scooped end looked like a tiny spoon. Said sadist would take said wooden rod and place it on exact pressure points, somehow eliciting mind-numbing pain.

In my head, I nicknamed him the Wooden Acupuncturist of Seoul. I tried to laugh through it; I tried to grit through the pain, but the fatigue set in.

They alternated questions with jolts of electricity and presses from the Wooden Acupuncturist. At some point, and I don't know when, Schultz got me to admit that I didn't have a contract. There was no employer. Avery and I had been working on our own.

That seemed to satisfy him for a brief period and he ordered himself a traditional American breakfast to be prepared and served right in front of me. French toast made of brioche bread, three eggs over easy, quarter-inch thick bacon, and two glasses of orange juice. I don't know if he did it because he had a thing for American brunch or if he was trying to elicit some kind of nostalgia. Either way, it was impossible to ignore the smell, to close my eyes to the sight. Such a small thing, yet, it twisted me towards his intentions.

He took his time eating, chatting amiably. He talked about the current status of the financial markets, the stupidity of the government in North Korea, and even lectured me on the lessons he'd learned as an entrepreneur.

I watched him through the haze, my mind trying to calculate. It was like pistons firing out of sequence. I tried to fall back on old lessons. The sleepless nights during hell week in

Coronado. The overnights of missions deep into enemy territory. But sadly, nothing had prepared me for this.

Schultz wiped his mouth. I don't know why, but I'll never forget that gesture. He did it slowly, carefully, dabbing at the corners like he expected a chef to wheel in a cart of his favorite dessert next. No dessert came. I was dessert.

The leftover food was removed and Schultz stood. He smiled at me once then looked up at the camera. I knew what that meant, even in my incapacitated state. I knew what was coming: Phase Three.

So I dove down, deep down into my being. I reached out for anything to grab and hold onto, something to ground me. What I found wasn't a thing, it wasn't a lesson, it wasn't even a memory. It was a person.

It was The Admiral, my father, the mean old cuss who'd given the finger to the Navy on his way out the door. I could see him as clear as day in my mind's eye. When I opened my real eyes, he was still there, standing in the corner with his arms crossed, watching me like he'd watched me all those years on the football field.

"You can do this," he said.

I gritted my teeth and shivered involuntarily.

Four men entered the room carrying more tools for my torture.

But even the sight of my father wasn't enough. He might have been watching, but when the interrogation began in earnest, when Phase Three locked in for forward progress, I was swept up in the tsunami and the old man vanished.

Seconds bled into hours. Pain bled into tears unbidden. Memories came and went. Strange things, like the time mother and I had flown from Yokosuka, Japan, to Seoul to visit my father. I remembered thinking that the hotel we stayed in was the most luxurious place I'd ever been. I ate chocolate donuts for every meal as we waited for my father who never came. He'd been sent off to some hotspot again. It was just my mother and me.

That memory faded and blended in with the rest. Currents of excruciating electricity coursed through my veins into my nerves. Then they attacked my pressure points, assailed my body with their perfectly placed blows.

They came and went. I have no idea for how long. Days? Months?

Sometimes, I got a glimpse of Baxter standing, watching from the back of the room right where my father had been. And sometimes he wasn't there. A blank wall in my blank life.

Not that it mattered. He was one of them. They were all the same, and I was alone. My only hope was that Avery had gotten out, that Schultz had told me the truth about releasing her. It was just about the only lucid hope I had left..

Finally, when I was sure I was breaths away from my own demise, I glanced in the corner and I saw the image of my father again. Shultz had been asking the same questions over and over. Why, why had I done it? Why had I targeted their organization? Why had I killed their minions? I tried screaming back, laughing in their faces, spitting on their shoes. The questions kept coming, and my father kept watching.

This time as I gazed at my father, his visage crystal clear, he nodded and said in a tone that only I could hear, "You've done enough son. You can tell them now."

Another jolt of electricity racked my body. It felt like my spine would snap in two. The current finally subsided. I was through, there was nowhere left to hide. I was broken, beaten down, a raw lump of human flesh.

"This can all end now," Schultz said soothingly.

Many times he said that exact phrase, but this time, I looked up wearily.

"Tell me, Tom, tell me why you did it."

And because my father said I could, I told him. I told him everything.

About Ella and Caleb.

The pain was worse than anything physical I had experienced in that room. I would have taken a year's worth of shocks over that.

But somehow, that retelling set me free.

It all came out in the interrogation room. But something else came out too: a little bit of regret and a lot of the pain, the byproduct of holding that story inside myself, like an alcoholic finally admitting that he had a problem.

The burden on my shoulders shifted, and somewhere through bleary eyes I knew that everything had changed, and that my mission was not yet over. I would avenge their deaths, or I would die trying.

FINALITY

The re-telling of my children's story had a calming affect on me. It brought my body back down to level and cleared my eyes enough to allow me to take in the room. The story apparently sobered witnesses as well.

During the pain and delirium, I hadn't noticed the crowd that Schultz had gathered. As the senior man, Schultz stood out from the others, closest to me. But I counted at least ten men standing in back of him including Agent Baxter. Nobody moved. They were all waiting for their cue from Schultz.

Finally, he spoke.

"Now we understand one another, Mr. Greer. If I had known your pain, I would've snuffed it out long ago." He shook his head and moved closer. "It would be condescending of me to say that I understand how you feel. To lose two children in one fell swoop, it is.... Well, I'm not a monster, Mr. Greer."

He shook his head sadly.

"I do know, however, what you must think of our underworld business dealings. Nefarious? Maybe. Distasteful? To some. But it fills a need, an insatiable hunger bred in to us by whatever almighty power put us upon this world." He exhaled like it was too much to consider. "But enough about that. No sense in opening that wound again. I would like to applaud you, Mr. Greer. A lesser man might have collapsed and let life take him. But you stood up. You overcame. You tracked us down one by one. There's something almost chivalrous about it, the shining knight avenging the death of his king, or his progeny. Oh, how I love the fairytales, King Arthur and his Knights of the Round Table. Noble and pure. But, in the end, their own weaknesses became their undoing." He motioned to me with a sweeping gesture. "But what am I saying? The man sitting before us today has no weaknesses that I can see. Your pursuit was just. It is a shame that your revenge will not be complete."

The men behind Schultz shifted in anticipation. The mob was eager for the judge's ruling. I ignored them and stared at Schultz who went on again.

"Your tenacity is commendable. Therefore, for what you've lost and what you've had to endure, my associates and I will not gather every last family member you have and skewer them along the ramparts. They are safe. And you? You've earned your warrior's death, Mr. Greer, and I salute you."

He looked down at his watch. "I'm afraid I must say goodbye for the last time. It has been an honor, truly, a privilege to have known you, to have spent this time with you." He turned to the assembly. "Gentlemen, I would like my friend from the FBI to do the honors. In for a penny, in for a pound, as they say."

He winked once at the crowd and once at me, then bowed and then left the room. And this time he was gone for good.

There were no slaps, no punches, no more jolts of electricity. When they picked my body up from the chair, their hands were gentle, reverent.

This time, the cell they took me to was clean and comfortable. There was a dome camera in one corner of the ceiling and a bed with actual sheets on the other side of the room. They deposited me on the bed and one of the goons said, "Mr. Schultz told us to prepare one last meal. Do you have a preference?"

"Chocolate donuts," I said, "and a glass of milk."

"Very well. Don't try to kill yourself. We're watching," the man said, unnecessarily pointing to the camera in the corner. "You do anything that looks like a suicide attempt, we start over."

I laid back on the bed as they left. My body was weak, but I felt my strength returning. I'm not sure if it was the act of removing my inner pain or just that I could actually see the finish line. Maybe I couldn't get to Schultz. Maybe I could.

What I did know was the next time someone came in, I was going to tear their heart out with my teeth and take as many along for the ride as I could.

* * *

THE DOOR LOCK CLICKED AND MY EYES SNAPPED OPEN. Agent Baxter walked in, easing the door closed behind him. He took his time coming to me, my own personal Death Eater.

He stood facing me, his back to the camera.

"I'd like to second Mr. Schultz's congratulations. You've come a long way, Tom. You even fooled me and that's not an easy thing to do. I bet you wish you would've killed me. God knows you had many chances. If only you'd known..."

He went on, but I wasn't listening to the words. I was staring at his chest where he held up a 3 x 5 index card with one hand. The camera and its operator couldn't see it, but I could.

The message was simple and to the point. "*I'm getting you out*," the neat handwriting read. "*Nod if you understand.*"

I sat up slowly, looked Baxter in the eye and nodded.

THE BREAK

The note in Baxter's hand disappeared quickly. For a split second, I thought I had imagined it, especially when he pulled the pistol out of his holster and screwed on a cylindrical suppressor.

"Mr. Schultz doesn't like loud noises. To be honest, I don't like making a mess." He bent over and shoved the end of the suppressor under my chin. "Do you get me?" He said this in a voice just above a whisper. I didn't respond.

Baxter let go of my chin and walked around me slowly, going on and on about the benefits of working for the FBI and the international syndicate. On his second pass around, his hand grazed mine and I felt him slip something into my palm. I clamped down on it. It was a key, a handcuff skeleton key.

Baxter kept pacing, kept talking. I didn't have time to think about whether it was another trap, another mind game. When you're in the middle of a shit sandwich, all you want to do, all you think about, is getting out.

Baxter was explaining how he'd been recruited and why he made the move when the first handcuff clicked off. The second followed, and I relished the immediate satisfaction of a few inches of released tension on my shoulders. They hadn't secured my feet, probably because they appeared to be of no use. They'd dragged me in and out of interrogations, like a limp rag doll. But I wasn't as useless as they thought. My flexing leg muscles were a testament to that fact.

Baxter stopped in front of me, his back once again to the camera. He said loud enough for someone to hear, "Where do you want it, Tom? In the forehead?" He pressed the barrel to my forehead. "Or how about in the temple?" He shifted the weapon around to my temple. I flexed my arms and my hands, trying to relieve the tingling. "No, I'll bet you want one right in the mouth. Don't you?" Baxter said. "Open your mouth," he ordered. I could imagine the men in the recording booth, pressed forward in anticipation. I opened my mouth and clamped down on the end of the barrel, feeling two loose teeth wiggle expectantly.

"You're a disgrace," Baxter said. "You're lucky Schultz made that promise. I wouldn't have made that promise." I was looking right up at him. His words said one thing, but his facial expressions said the exact opposite. There was something bordering on compassion there, or maybe it was expectation. "*Do it*," that face said.

My hands moved to the back of my thighs now. For the camera, it looked like I was still bound and secured.

"It's your time, Tom. Tick-tock," Baxter said. Then looking right at me, he mouthed the words, "*Do it*."

When I made my move, it felt like I was moving my body through sludge. My left hand came out and caught the pistol, yanking it from my mouth, while my right came across and clocked Baxter in the jaw. He sprawled out easily. Before I could relish my victory, he looked back at me and then to the camera. He yelled, "Get him!"

I pivoted, took aim on the camera. One shot and the

thing was disabled, crackling and spitting sparks in frustration. I put my back to the wall on one side of the door.

"You have five seconds before they come in," Baxter said. "There are two guards in the video room. Take them out. I'll see what I can do to cover you."

"Why?" I asked, meaning why was he helping me. He seemed to understand.

"Maybe we'll discuss it over a beer later."

The door slammed open. One man rushed in. I put a bullet in the back of his head. His body crumpled. The second man followed, tripping over his companion. My first shot hit the man in the back. My hands still weren't working right. The second shot took him in the left temple. His weapon skittered across the floor.

Baxter was on his feet now.

"There's a locker room down the hall," he said. "I left a uniform hanging for you. It should fit. Get dressed and get out of here."

"What about you?" I asked.

"I can handle myself. Now go." There was no time for thanks, no time for questions. Baxter was an enigma. He always had been. Maybe I would see him again. And then again, maybe I wouldn't. I was halfway out the door before he said, "Check in the left pocket of the uniform blouse. It's Avery's new number," he said.

I nodded and slipped down the quiet hallway in nothing but my boxer briefs, spattered and stained with my own blood and filth. I don't know how I got to the locker room. My body dragged like I'd run a marathon every day for a month. But I had to hurry. I didn't know how much time I had.

When I entered the empty locker room, I happened to glance in the mirror over the sink. I took in my haggard appearance. My muscles sagged and deep lines had formed on my weathered face. There was good news. I looked into my own eyes and I saw the fire that I had felt in that room. I felt the power within me rising again. It was all the motivation I needed to slip into the janitor's uniform. Baxter had been kind enough to leave me a pair of socks and work boots as well. Sixty seconds after entering the locker room, I was dressed.

I grabbed a towel from the hook next to the sink and wrapped the silenced pistol, then I snagged a blue ball cap lying on the bench, one of those numbers with the circular crown. I pulled it low to cover my eyes. I left the locker room, scanning the hallway but no one was there. No one at all. Had that been Baxter's doing?

I got that creeping sensation you get when someone tells you, "Coast is clear," but you know the boogeymen are ready to jump from the shadows.

No monsters sprang forth as I hurried down the hall towards the exit sign.

Just get outside.

I creaked the door open an inch, just in case. It was dark outside. I honestly hadn't known whether it was morning or night. The starless, moonless sky covered my exit. I left without a word, but my head was recalibrating, pistons firing in sync once again.

I slipped into the night and thought about one thing and one thing only: how I was going to kill Marco Schultz and his compatriots.

SAM'S YOUR MAN

One week.

Avery told me I had been in the syndicate's clutches for a whole week. God, it had felt like a year. I had called her on a phone that I borrowed from a kind elderly husband and wife who were on vacation from Tulsa, Oklahoma. She told me quickly that Baxter had grilled her the entire way home.

"I don't think you should trust him, Tom," she said in a shaky voice, "I think he's playing both sides."

"You're going to be okay," I said. She didn't question my using *you're* instead of *we're*. Was it something in my voice? "While we're on the subject, how are you?"

"I can't sleep. I keep thinking they're gonna come get me, that they're watching me right now. But I've checked everywhere, just like you taught me. No cameras. No bugs. I'm at my fourth Airbnb since getting back to the States."

"Good." I said. "You remember what I told you. If you need to disappear, you do it."

"But, Tom—"

"No buts, Avery. You take care of yourself. You know how. Now, let's get back down to business."

Despite being kidnapped, imprisoned, and tortured, Avery's mind slipped back into our old routine. *Good girl*, I thought. *Stay busy.*

She told me how she had accessed the old network, how she watched Schultz come and go, how she'd kept tabs on the final target.

"It's Baxter who I don't get," she said.

"What do you mean?"

"I catch glimpses of him leaving that building, the one where they had you, but that's all. He leaves and he just disappears. I told you, I don't trust him." Her voice was shaking again.

"Easy, I'll take care of it. Okay? Now, let's get back to the seven."

"Okay," she said meekly and then stronger, "Alright." Her voice brightened, "I think we lucked out. There's going to be a meeting. They're all going to be there."

"Tell me where."

"Tom, do you think you're up for it? I mean—"

"I'll be fine."

There was a long pause, as if she was deciding whether to give me that final piece of information. Whether she knew it spelled my imminent demise, I can't be sure. She finally told me where Schultz and his bosses were meeting.

"Be careful, Tom."

"You know I always am. And Avery?"

"Yeah?"

"Thank you. For everything."

I ended the call before she could say another word. I took a deep breath, and handed the cell phone back to its owner.

"Is everything all right?" the woman asked.

"Just fine, thanks."

"You don't look fine."

"I just had a bad bowl of kimchi. Got my stomach pretty good. A week in a hotel bed."

Woman jabbed an elbow into her husband's side, "See, I told you we should've brought our own snacks. Now, give the young man the money he asked for."

The old man grumbled, fished some bills from his pocket.

"Thank you," I said, taking the money and slipping it into the pocket of the oversized shorts I'd taken from a neighborhood clothesline. "Like I said, contact my airline and give them my name."

"Captain Thomas Greer," the woman repeated.

"That's right. I put the phone number in your contacts."

"But where will you go?"

"I have to go see some old friends and repay an old debt."

I left them to wonder, and headed for a part of town that only the locals frequented. I was in need of a shower, shave, and a new suit. That, and a few party favors for the night's festivities.

* * *

I only knew the proprietor as Sam. Sam had been orphaned during the Korean War. He might've been lost to time if it hadn't been for the US Navy Seabees who'd taken the five-year-old and made him sort of an unofficial mascot of their post-war outpost. As the Seabees came and went, one rotation replacing the previous watch-standers, Sam stayed, always working, always learning.

His English was decidedly Midwestern, not a hint of an accent, and he spoke his native tongue fluently, along with Mandarin, Japanese, and a touch of Russian.

At the age of 18, Sam had been recruited by the CIA, thanks to a heavy list of recommendations from the Naval

Construction Battalion outpost. He spent the next three decades slipping in and out of North Korea, providing much needed intel to the United States government. He'd earned a tidy pension for his efforts.

Since retiring, he'd opened a custom tailor shop deep inside the largest market in Korea. I'd been introduced to Sam by a SEAL friend who'd gone to work for the Agency.

"If you ever need a good suit, Sam's the best. And if you ever find yourself in a tight spot, Sam's your man."

And my friend was right. The second I stepped into his shop, the spy-turned-suit-maker rose from the sewing machine, arms out wide.

"Tom, it's so good to see you." But then he really saw my appearance. "But what happened?" He stopped short, looking me up and down.

"I got into a little trouble, nothing I couldn't handle."

He decided not to press, and instead extended a leathery hand, "How can I help you, my friend?"

"I need a suit, Sam, and some accessories."

Sam grinned. "You know what they say?"

"Sam's your man," we said in unison.

For the next hour, Sam barked orders at his team of seamstresses. They took my measurements and floated fabric by so I could choose the right pattern. It didn't really matter to me, but if this was going to be the last suit I was ever going to wear, I might as well go out in style.

He had his staff bring me food. All my stomach could take was broth and white rice. Not one of Sam's people blinked twice when I had to throw up in the trashcan. All Sam said was, "You need to take better care of yourself, Tom."

When the measurements and selections were finished, he patted me on the shoulder and said, "Come with me. Let's see to your accessories."

We went up a flight of stairs and then down another. Sam

didn't only own the modest storefront that he housed his tailor shop in, but he also owned half a block, and each tenant knew him by name. He waved as we passed, not one of his friends giving us a second look.

Finally, we came to a decrepit storage room. Sam took a key from his pocket, undid the padlock, and we stepped inside. Once he had padlocked us in on the other side, we went down one last set of steps.

"Heavy or light?" he asked nonchalantly, like a soda jerk asking for flavor preferences.

"Light," I said.

"On person? Or will you be taking luggage?"

"I prefer not to have to carry anything."

Sam nodded, sifting through inventory in his head.

We came to a set of double metal doors, only this one didn't have a simple padlock. One of the doors was inset within another metal cabinet, like the ones they have at the doctor's office where you place your pee cup for urine tests.

Sam opened the small door, and the facial recognition screen lit up. Sam put his face close and said, "Sam's your man."

I watched the program go from red to green, then the pneumatic lock on the door plunked open. We stepped inside the massive vault and lights came on all around us.

"Impressive," I said, looking around the room at the display cases. "This is new?"

"I've been busy."

"Business is good, then?"

"The suit business or the accessory business?" Sam walked over to one particularly ominous rack and lifted a Barrett .50 caliber out of the display case. "Both businesses are good, although my margins on the accessories are significantly higher. Now, as much as I'd love to give you this," he patted the Barrett lovingly, "you said that you were in the market for lighter fare. Might I suggest the case to your left?"

I turned and smiled, marveling at the array of weaponry my Korean friend had stockpiled.

"You never cease to amaze me, Sam." I handed him a thin sheet of paper. "Call that number. They'll take care of my tab."

He waved the paper away. "I know you're good for it, Tom. You'll pay me later."

"Take it, Sam, just in case."

Sam studied me with those eyes that had seen untold atrocities north of the DMZ. He'd saved countless lives, and probably helped us avert nuclear war on more than one occasion. He finally took the slip of paper, and his countenance returned to that of congenial shopkeeper.

"Now, as you'll see over here..." He had every caliber anyone could ever want: slim, bulky, silenced, not. "This drawer holds my latest acquisitions." He opened it, and I looked inside. "Any of these fit the bill?"

I nodded and started making my selections.

THE BATMOBILE

S am had done his very best. I was showered, shaved, and wrapped in his perfectly tailored suit. The compartments were so expertly made, that when I turned around in front of the mirror, I couldn't detect a single bulge from any of my weapons.

"There you go, you look good," Sam said. "But, your face! Are you sure you don't want—?"

"I don't want any makeup," I told Sam for the fifth time. I'm sure his salon lady was still waiting. "What do I look like, a model? Besides, it's going to be dark."

He shrugged and did one last pass around me, picking off pieces of lint that I couldn't see, and smoothing out minuscule creases like I was some prize pony going to the big show.

"Do you have friends going with you?" he asked.

It was the first time he'd asked about what I was doing, even though I'd volunteered my destination and arrival window. Sam never pressed, whether it was my condition or that he sensed some change in me. The truth is, he was concerned, plain and simple. One human being caring for another. He patted me on the back and said, "Never mind, forget I asked. But if you need help, call me. The cell phone I gave you has my number programmed." Before I could protest, he put up a hand, "Don't worry. If anything happens to you, the call goes through a series of relays. If the system doesn't hear your voice, the call is sent to another one of my businesses."

Clever Sam, I thought.

From orphan to spy supplier.

Sam looked down at his watch, "You better get going, Tom, and here." He produced a key fob.

"What's this?"

"I know the club you're going to. Unless you're on the list, you need to make a splash to get in."

I took the key and shook my head, "Maybe it would be easier if I snuck in."

"Maybe," Sam said, "but this way is more fun. Come, I'll walk you out."

When we stepped out of Sam's store, a crowd of street urchins was gathered around a black mass parked on the street. Sam snapped out something in Korean, and the children scattered.

I recognized the vehicle immediately: a USSV Rhino GX. Built in California, the oversized SUV was equal parts armored personnel carrier and luxury family mover. It was massive and imposing and, knowing Sam, probably upgraded.

"I can't take that thing, Sam."

"Trust me." Sam pushed me to the car door. I could feel the heft of the thing as the portal opened, courtesy of one of Sam's seamstresses. I slipped inside, admiring the impressive array of electronics and the rich scent of luxurious leather. "There, now you look like Bruce Wayne," Sam said.

I chuckled modestly. "I really can't take this. Sam, it's a $250,000 car."

Sam shook his head, "More like half a million, with upgrades."

"Well now I definitely can't take it."

He actually shushed me, waving an impatient hand in my face. "If you must know, it belonged to a competitor. I have no need for it. So, if something were to happen..."

"I'll make sure you get it back," I said, even though I was in no position to make such a promise.

"Now go," Sam said. "You don't want to be late."

He closed me inside, and I pressed the starter button. The engine came to life, equal parts purr and rumble, like a sleeping panther. In another time and place, I would've popped open the hood and checked inside, examined the wheel wells, and then maybe taken it off road. But there was no time for that now. I rolled down the window and waved to Sam and his team. Then I put the beast into drive, and eased my way out of the neighborhood.

Bruce Wayne, indeed, I thought to myself. I couldn't help grinning as I left to join the party.

THE DMZ

I got to DMZ beats after midnight. I'm not talking about the De-Militarized Zone. I'm talking about the three-story club outfitted like it was the real DMZ. Drab gray paint. Bold streaks of red piping.

I pulled to the roped-off curb, gawkers scattering. A gorilla-sized bouncer in a North Korean military uniform stepped out with the authority of a commanding general. I was already out of the vehicle and onto the sidewalk when I handed him the key as if I didn't care what happened to the car.

"You can't park here," he said.

I gave him my best billionaire glare. "I'm late."

He took a step closer. "And I don't know you," he said, his demeanor a touch lighter than his initial greeting. He was my height but twice as broad.

I smiled smarmily. "I have a date. She's waiting inside."

Any further protest was cutoff when he saw what I was holding in my hand: five crisp one-hundred-dollar bills folded as neat as bed sheets at Parris Island.

He took the money and then snapped his fingers. Two North Korean-clad soldiers appeared.

"Take our guest to the second level and make sure he's searched," the ogre said.

"Searched?" I said, feigning amusement.

My escorts were much more gracious than their ring-leader. Rather than words, they used grunts to get me past the winding line of prospective guests, most of whom would never get in the exclusive club.

We entered through a door to the left of the main entrance. There was a dark hallway inside that smelled of high-end perfume and cigarettes.

"In here," one of them said, pointing to a parlor whose door was half-open. I stepped inside and they followed, closing the door behind us.

"Take off your jacket," one of them said.

"I'm not taking off my jacket," I said imperiously. "Unless you put a dollar in my G-string."

Neither cracked a smile. I produced two additional hundred dollar bills. Still nothing. I'm not sure if they were used to bribes or were afraid of the ogre outside.

"Jacket," the other one said, pointing from me to the chair in the corner.

I slipped the cash back in my pocket and came out brandishing something much more useful than money.

There was no time for them to react. With one smooth pull, I lifted the suppressed weapon to eye level.

The first round took one in the forehead and the second in the temple. They collapsed in muted thumps.

"Sorry, boys," I said.

I stepped around their bodies, careful to avoid the blood oozing onto the carpet.

Eerie blue light illuminated the shadowy hallway. I

followed the sound of thumping bass to the door at the end of the hall.

The first floor was the club for the commoners, the people who had to wait outside. There were booths on elevated platforms surrounding the dance floor packed with guests guzzling expensive champagne. More than a few booths held commoners that would not remember the night's festivities. They slumped and snored, foreshadows of the hangovers to come.

But *my* targets didn't mingle with commoners.

I ascended the grand gilded stairway that led to a set of double doors on the second floor. No North Korean wannabes blocked the way, and I didn't sense any eyes on me - for now anyway.

I pulled the heavy doors open. There was another set of double doors inside, and these were manned by more guards in uniforms. They eyed me casually, but when I strode forward, they did not stop me. Why? Because I didn't act like the commoners on level one.

They opened the door, and I strode past them into the second level. Here the music was more 1920s New York. The waitresses were all topless and did as much carousing as they did serving. This level catered to high-end businessmen from Tokyo and Hong Kong, among other places. The clientele was decidedly Asian, although I caught glimpses of a raucous pair of Russians in one corner, and a disheveled looking group who I guessed were Germans in one smoke-filled alcove.

A cigarette lady who was as naked as her co-workers confronted me.

"Cigarettes, sir?" she gestured grandly to her tray of goods, if you know what I mean.

"How much?"

"Twenty for the cigarettes, ten for the drink."

I pointed to a box of cigarettes and gave her a twenty along with a hefty tip. "Lighter?" I asked.

"Matches," she said with a smile, producing them from her waistband.

I tapped a cigarette from the package and put it to my lips. She lit it for me and then handed me the rest of the matches.

"Thank you," I said. "I'm late for a meeting."

"Oh?" she asked lasciviously.

I wondered idly if all the women on this floor were available for rent.

"One of the doorman from downstairs was supposed to escort me to the third level, but he got detained." One of her eyebrows arched unconvinced. "A group of Australian rugby players wouldn't leave your co-workers alone."

Now she nodded. "I saw them earlier, very rude. Too much to drink," and she looked around slowly to see if my phantom escort had arrived.

"Look," I said, "if you don't get me to that meeting, I'm out fifty million dollars. You don't want that on your conscience, do you?"

Her eyes said it all.

She wasn't supposed to let anyone up to the third floor. No one was. But fifty million dollars meant that I must have at least a portion of that on my person.

She waited knowing that she didn't have to ask. The two bills I'd tried to give to the dead men downstairs came out again.

"Double," she said without looking at them. Another two bills slipped onto her tray and she sucked them up like a Hoover. Then she gave me one last up and down as if she had X-ray vision to ensure I was no threat. If asked, she would probably say she'd never seen me. She knew as well as I did that there were no cameras on levels two and three. Paying guests demanded discretion.

But nobody in this joint was above making some extra cash. She'd just made as much as she probably earned on her best night unless, of course, she was a worker of the extra-curricular brand.

Her eyes flicked to the far side of the smoky expanse. She rearranged the items on her tray, as if she was still selling them to me. "Staircase in the back hall," she said. Then she cocked her head to the side and smiled. "Sam says 'hello and be careful.'"

I was too shocked to respond. Before I could say anything, she was gone, peddling her wares and spying for Sam. I had to laugh.

I found the door without incident and stood to one side finishing my cigarette, waiting for the perfect moment. No eyes on me. I made my move.

I slipped inside, stumbling through on purpose. There was a guard inside; another North Korean replica. This one was actually carrying an AK-47, although it was hanging from a strap over his shoulder. He looked up in surprise from his phone.

I banged into the wall. "This isn't the bathroom," I slurred, flicking my cigarette at his feet.

"No entry," he said stiffly as if he'd rehearsed it for the last two hours.

I grinned like a drunken fool, wobbling on my feet.

"Pee pee in the toilet," I slurred grabbing my crotch and swaying comically.

He finally got the joke and even grinned a little bit, pointed back the way I'd come.

"Oh," I said throwing my arms in the air as if I'd realized my mistake. But with my momentum I fell forward and he reached out, not with one, but with two arms to catch me.

Bad move, fake soldier.

He caught me just as I clasped my hands behind his neck. And before he could call out an alarm, I drove my knee so hard into his midsection that it lifted him off the floor. He was warm putty in my hands after that. The moaning was easily drowned out by the music coming from all sides. I wrapped an anaconda arm around his neck and squeezed until he lost consciousness.

I was lucky enough to find a janitor's closet at the end of the alcove. I stashed the limp guard, hastily secured and gagged. I thought about taking the AK-47, but instead removed the magazine and emptied the chamber, disposing the rounds in a murky mop bucket. Then I headed for the stairs leading to the third level.

I fished out another cigarette and lit it. I didn't really know what I would find. Even Sam couldn't tell me what was on the third floor, but what I saw in the room when I stepped through the door of the third level was far from what I expected. Instead of a continuation of the debauchery of levels one and two, tier three was all corporate business and polished glass. It was like an elevated version of one of those shared office suites. But here things felt more, well, expensive, like the walls were made of gold. Here there were deals in the billions being done, offers for corporate takeover and life or death decisions.

There was a bank of elevators at the far end. Probably the way I should have come up. I recognized my mistake when a trio of guards saw me and headed my way. I walked towards them, right hand in my pocket, my left still holding the cigarette to my lip, as I took one last drag. Then I blew the smoke out, trying to buy time, steadying myself for the coming act.

I hadn't seen who I'd come for yet. Maybe Avery was wrong. If only she was ever wrong.

The three guards kept coming, and there were at least ten more posted around the cavernous room. Not easy, but not impossible either. As long as I found Shultz and his cohorts.

I was about to say something to the approaching security team, but the words stuck in my throat as I looked over their shoulders and saw a man coming off the elevator, a man who locked eyes with me and didn't falter. He didn't register an ounce of shock.

Marco Shultz stared at me. He shook his head and smiled.

Behind Shultz, Ned Baxter stepped off the elevator and I knew I'd been had.

CHAOS

The entire room froze, but as the witnesses gawked, I planned out my shots. The most immediate threat was the three guards, who were now six feet from me. Tap, tap, tap. Maybe an extra shot apiece. Then chaos would reign.

I would take as many out as I needed, as long as I got Schultz and his boss. I hadn't seen the almighty bigwig yet, but I had seen a cluster of security guards in the far left corner from me, the only ones who'd been sharp and alert from the start.

"Impressive, Mr. Greer," Schultz said. "Agent Baxter gave you three days. I said two. You beat all our expectations. Congratulations."

He waited for me to speak.

Sorry, Bub. I've done enough talking.

"Get them all out," Schultz barked, when he'd grown tired of waiting. Security details ushered the frightened patrons out the door, millionaires staring in shock. Billionaires staring with glee. But the group of guards in the far corner never moved. They didn't even budge. Well-trained centurions, they stood their ground.

The evacuation was done swiftly and without incident. When the elevator dinged for the final time, Schultz spoke again.

"There's no way out, you know. You should have taken the shot when you could." Again he waited for me to speak. "Ah, still no words. But you were so eloquent days ago. I miss that, Mr. Greer. And to be honest, I've missed you." He looked around the room and then back at me. "But before you die, I'm sure you'd like to know the truth. Think back, Mr. Greer. Do you really think it would have been so easy to escape? Your own children were swallowed up like inconsequential gnats. What made you think that you, a washed up old warrior, could somehow be so lucky as to have a friend on the inside?" Schultz put his arm around Baxter. "He's mine, Mr. Greer. And he's told me everything."

"Why?" I asked. And they both knew the question was directed at Baxter.

Schultz nodded, releasing his muzzled dog to speak.

"You're an unfortunate side effect, Tom," Baxter said. "I was sorry to hear about your children. But that was a long time ago. Things have changed. Assurances have been made. There's no need to be in the ugly side of the business anymore. One hundred percent legitimacy is our goal."

I'm not sure whether he was trying to sell me or just explain it in his logical robotic way. To me, it sounded like a bad riff on Michael Corleone's story in *The Godfather*. But just like in that story, I knew the truth. No business born of murder could ever truly wash their hands of the stain.

Call me old-fashioned, or just plain stupid, but I wanted to know the truth.

"Why did you do it?"

"I don't know what answer you're looking for, Tom," said Baxter. "But I'll tell you why I did it. Money and power. Plain and simple."

Shultz spread his arms as if Baxter had just lain down the word of God.

Now I saw the guards in the corner shuffling, like an agitated brood of hens, sensing the fox in the henhouse.

"There, you have your answer," Schultz said. "Now, I'm afraid I must ask you to leave. Escort him out," he barked to the three men who hadn't taken their eyes from me.

Enough of the bullshit, I thought. I went straight to the ground, pulling my silenced pistol as I moved. The men got three steps closer and two of them went down with shots in the leg. They crumpled and the third man kept coming. Either he was fanatical or just stupid. There was no weapon in his hand.

Two feet.

I sprang to my feet, and my hand cupped around the other item I'd pulled from a hidden pocket: Sam's secret stash.

The guard lunged for me, but I went into a squat. I hammered him in the midsection with my closed fist. Then, I grabbed his waistband as he slumped forward and shoved something in the front of his pants.

I counted down: *five, four…*

The man looked down frantically, still out of breath, his face puffed and swollen.

Three…

I spun around and kicked him in the ass, pushing his away from me.

No one else had seen what I had done, but they were about to feel it.

Two… one.

I dropped to the floor again, just in time, as the explosive no larger than a cigarette lighter turned the staggering guard into a bursting blood balloon. I pulled three more explosives from my pocket and threw them into the glass conference rooms as the others cowered.

Baxter had shielded Schultz, but they were both covered in blood. The FBI agent was cursing.

The guards in the corner were moving now.

Three, two, one.

Blammo! The explosives ripped through the room, daggering glass, spreading the expanse with jagged shrapnel. Some glass hit me in the arms and legs, but the material that Sam used to craft my expensive attire held.

There was a mad rush for the elevator now, the hens carrying someone in their midst: *Target Number Seven.*

More men poured out from hidden alcoves I hadn't seen and staircases I hadn't noticed.

If Schultz was frightened, he didn't show it.

"Get him," he yelled. I ran to close the distance between us, taking out one, two, three, four guards.

I almost slipped on the blood on the tile.

Five.

Out of rounds.

I pulled a second pistol from the inside pocket of my suit coat.

Rounds were coming my way now. I felt one hit me in the meaty part of my thigh. I winced. Still, the reinforced fabric held.

Baxter and Schultz were forty feet away now. I know what you're thinking. Just shoot, Tom. It's only forty feet. Sorry. There was something I wanted, no, *needed* to do. I needed to get up close and personal. I wanted to see the life drain from the hypocrites' eyes, both of them.

But then another round hit me in the side. They were coming from all around.

The elevator dinged. Target Number Seven was gone.

Desperation spurned me on. Baxter backpedaled, the FBI agent shielding his boss as best he could.

Shots all around, smoke rising. One fire alarm went off and then another. The lights flickered off and on several times before they went out.

I pressed forward, taking down everyone in my path. I saw a man rushing at me from the left. I pulled a knife from the sheath in my waistband, threw it without looking. I heard the grunt through the cacophony as the blade hit him in the chest.

I had Baxter in my sights now. Maybe two or four more shots, and it would be done. A valiant effort. Number Seven was gone. Perhaps Avery would pick up the fight.

Avery.

I said a silent prayer for her and for her life, for innocence lost. I was to blame.

I never finished this thought. A ground-shaking explosion scattered us like bowling pins to the floor.

I looked behind me to where I thought the sound originated, although I couldn't be sure. I almost shook my head in disbelief. Emerging from the smoke was the cigarette girl, Sam's plant from downstairs. She entered the room with a casual step, not unlike her sales gig on level two. But now instead of the cigarette tray, she held an automatic weapon to her shoulder, above her bare breasts. And she had friends. Two more waitresses accompanied her and they set about mowing through the enemy.

The building was still disgorging fake North Korean soldiers like rats in a flooded subway system. One waitress went down and then another. I used the distraction to my advantage, moving forward again. But when I got ten feet from my quarry, I realized my mistake. Six magazines had come in with me and now six magazines had been expended. I dropped the pistol to the ground and pulled the CRKT blade from my wrist sheath. It was made in Chattanooga, Tennessee, a place I'd never see again. *To the death*, I thought, as I closed the remaining feet.

But then another surprising thing happened. Just as I was reaching out to grab Schultz, the pair turned. Schultz's face registered surprise, but Baxter looked right at me, gun in hand.

"He's all yours," he said and pushed the German into my hands. He winked at me and ran toward the converging gun battle, firing like a madman.

So many questions, so little time. Baxter, a double agent? No. A triple agent?

Reality descended on Schultz like the Black Plague. He tried to run. I grabbed him by the back of the collar. There were no words to summarize what I felt for this man, just as there aren't adequate words to describe the pain he helped cause. So rather than whisper some sadistic lullaby in his ear, I let my blade do the talking. It plunged into his neck, at the base of his skull right where the spine connected to all those vital human components. He twitched like he'd been shot.

If only I'd had the time to watch him take his last breath, but I didn't. I kicked him away and ran for the exit of a once-hidden staircase whose door now lay ajar.

I took one look back in the room. The cigarette woman went down with a shot to the leg but kept firing at the advancing enemy. Baxter was reloading and then firing again.

There were too many of them. He'd given me just enough time. I didn't know his motives and it didn't really matter. I pushed through the door just as Baxter went down in a flurry of bullets.

No time to think on that now, Tom. Time to save your ass and track down Number Seven.

GOING DOWN

I'm not lying when I say that I went head over heels down the steps. Killing Schultz had taken something out of me and I think seeing Ned die did too.

And then there was my brain. Too many hits? Too many surprises?

Confusion laced with wonder. Why do people do what they do?

I didn't have time to think about that as I tried to arrest my fall. But at least the impromptu gymnastics had saved me. Lady Luck was still on my side. I was keenly aware of the rounds shattering the marble steps less than two feet from my head as I rolled by. More security guards were coming up from below, with no topless cigarette ladies to save me.

I tucked my body as well as I could and followed the momentum, ignoring the jarring pain, trying to do my best imitation of a Hollywood stunt double.

Shouts and smoke assaulted my senses. The discombobulation was punctuated by arrested momentum as I smacked into one particularly well-made wall at the far end of the landing. Through the haze, I could see them coming for me, their gray and red uniforms marching through the mist.

I wondered, for some reason, if that's what it would look like for our troops if they marched straight up through the real DMZ.

The building shook again. Luckily, I was on the floor this time. The rushing guards weren't so lucky, and they reached for stability wherever they could find it. I took this as my cue and jumped off the landing and into their midst punching, grabbing, slashing. I tore my way through them.

Their confusion was my temporary salvation. I slashed wrists and gouged eyes. A knee in the gut and an elbow in the nose. It was like setting a wildcat loose in a turkey pen.

I left them bleeding and dying, but not before picking up an automatic rifle and two pistols that I shoved in my pockets.

Chaos reigned down as I ran, ceiling tiles dislodged, and dry wall cracked and turned to dust. It was like a demolition crew had been sent to tear down the building without clearing the place of people.

When I burst onto the second level, all I heard was screaming and wailing fire alarms. It was impossible to see now. The smoke here was black and oozing like tar. I ran headlong into a pair of guards. I dispatched one with a knife to the carotid, and the other with a butt stroke to the face from my newly acquired weapon.

Relying solely on memory, I went down the last flight of stairs, pushing by terrified guests who were running and bleeding while others froze in sheer panic.

I tried to blend in, slipping through their ranks like a rogue fish in a school. Finally, the main entrance came into view. It was there that I saw it, the head of Target Number Seven passing under the archway and out to freedom.

I lifted the rifle and took aim, but there were too many

civilians in my way. Say what you want about me, I'm not a murderer of innocents.

I had to push my way through now, desperate to get to the one in charge. I elbowed and kneed, dashing through them, my panic rising.

If my target got in a car, it was all over. Seven would disappear. I'd be left standing amongst an army of my enemy.

Fresh air at last. Somehow I got through. Somehow I saw the top of that shiny black hair again.

I called out to get Seven's attention, but the surge of human bodies was too strong, screams too loud; echoes of blaring sirens engulfed us all.

There was a limousine at the curb, door open, escorts waiting. I raised the rifle again and took two well-aimed shots. More guards down. But now my view was obstructed again by the masses around me.

The crowd flinched from the shots and like that school of bait fish, they twisted away from danger. That was good and bad. It cleared the way, but my cover was gone.

In the next moment, I realized that my cover didn't matter. From somewhere overhead, from the roof or a helicopter maybe, came rattles of automatic gunfire. A string of people in front of me went down and then more collapsed to my side. Still the blaring, still the screaming.

I looked up at the night sky. Time slowed with the approach of the helo. There, in the open helicopter door, was a heavy caliber weapon trained on yours truly. I turned, thinking to engage it for no better purpose than to give me another ten seconds to reach Number Seven.

But then something streaked in from a rooftop across the street. The man and his mounted weapon disappeared in the ensuing explosion. The helicopter careened right, away from me, away from the crowd.

Now that we were past the exterior club barriers, people

scattered, eager to be gone from the violence. I saw my prize up ahead. They had reached the limousine. I raised my rifle again, took aim, perfect aim, deadly aim, impossible to miss, and depressed the trigger.

Click. Nothing.

I tried to clear the jam, ejecting a round from the side port.

Click again.

Dammit!

I threw the weapon to the ground and grabbed a pistol from my pocket. Number Seven was too far but I fired anyway, rounds dinging into the metal of the limousine. My target slipped into the limo and the vehicle was off before the doors closed.

I screamed in frustration, running now, taking guards down, not even thinking.

Bam Bam! Down.

Bam Bam! Down.

Bam Bam!

But the limousine streaked away.

I pulled out the other pistol and fired, two of the rounds catching the back window, which did nothing more than splinter.

I felt them more than I saw them now, the survivors closing in. Their emperor was gone and they had been left to dispose of the enemy.

Bring it on, you bastards!

I fired like a madman until my last magazine was expended. I'd been hit at least four times, the armored fabric still doing its work. But my body was failing me now. The old stubbornness could only take me so far. I'd been weakened and drained by my time in captivity. First, it was my left leg that cramped. Then, almost bowling me over, it was my right thigh. At least it felt like a cramp. Maybe it was another bullet.

This was it. The last of the enemy soldiers banded together. In a word, I was screwed.

Don't let them see your fear. My father's words echoed in my head. *Don't let them see your pain.*

Now, taking cover behind the squat concrete barrier, I had no rounds left, no more tricks up my sleeve, only the knife sitting in the palm of my right hand.

Taking on men that I'd stumbled across with the blade was one thing. Taking on a line of advancing soldiers was another.

What to do? Sit there and wait?

No.

I think you know by now that that's not my style. If I was going down, I was going to do it while looking them in the eye. This was it. Hell, six out of seven ain't bad. I hadn't won the World Series, but at least I'd done humanity some good by ridding it of its refuse.

I stood, holding my arms out wide. I felt a bullet zip by my ear. Another tore through my suit. The brave knight, his armor in tatters.

I closed my eyes and took a step from behind the barrier. I opened my arms wide.

Come and get me boys! Who's gonna be the big fat winner?

There was a loud *BOOM*.

It took me a long moment to realize what it was.

Another boom. One of the advancing line flew backwards. Boom again.

The shots were coming from the shadows to my right.

Boom! Boom!

I heard the racking of shotgun cartridges and turned.

I could just make out a hooded figure.

Sam? No. Too tall.

The line of guards shifted, half their weapons now trained on the mystery helper.

Boom!

Another one flew.

I picked another one off with a well-aimed throw of my blade.

Boom! Boom!

There was no time for them to react. Whatever coordination they had before was gone, destroyed by the deadly accuracy of the shotguns blasts.

Whoever the mystery savior was came closer.

Boom!

Now they really did scatter.

Boom! Another one down.

Boom! Boom!

My own private artillery barrage.

There was nothing left for me to finish by the time I got to them. They were either down and writhing, dead, or running.

The shotgun blasts had stopped. When I turned to face the mystery man, the figure was already floating away like an apparition. Positive that there were no threats left, I ran after him.

"Hey!"

He didn't turn, just kept walking. I saw the shotgun with an oversized drum magazine clatter to the ground.

The hooded figure kept walking.

I finally caught up to him and grabbed him by the shoulder. "Hey!"

I grabbed his shoulder. Just before he turned around, I noticed that the person was gray. It was a total shock when the man completed his turn. He was a man I knew well, the man who had brought me into this world.

My father.

The Admiral.

His eyes were blank as I stared at him through tear-filled eyes. And then he focused and searched my face.

"Tommy?"

"Dad, what are you...?"

"You found him!" Avery's lithe form appeared out of the darkness, followed closely by Sam who was cradling a shotgun identical to the one my father had dropped.

I was too shocked for words. I hadn't planned on making it out of the club, let alone seeing my friends again. And what about Dad, how had he... ?

"Oh, Tommy!" He patted me on the cheek, smiling despite the carnage all around us, the flashing lights of police cars arriving on the scene. "Tommy, I had the most wonderful dream!"

I wrapped one arm around him and the other around Avery, already heading away from any forthcoming questions of the local police.

"Come on, Dad. Let's go home."

EPILOGUE

Home.

What does that word mean to you?

A place to live?

A place to raise a family?

Or maybe just a place where you feel comfortable laying your head at night.

The word lost all meaning to me over the preceding years.

I know the dictionary definition.

> **Home:** *n.* the place where one lives permanently, especially as a member of a family or household

That definition connotes so much: permanence, family and belonging. Three things I didn't have, or at least things that I believed I had lost.

And yet, through the trappings of hell, grand things are born, seeds planted, new lives begun.

And so, despite the pain, despite what I'd endured, somehow I came out on the other end.

A miracle? Maybe.

Pure luck? I'm sure there was plenty to go around.

But if I had to sit back and read the entire episode with a dispassionate eye, I'd say it came down to friends and family, two things I thought I didn't have.

We traipse through life thinking we don't have an affect on others, when, in fact, we're all open hands in calm water. A single move, a casual wave, or an angry word, disrupts the world around us.

Ever heard of the butterfly effect? Well I have, and I think I believe in it now.

Tiny actions have the ability to turn into huge consequences.

Take me as an example. I'd befriended Avery, and yeah, we'd tracked down some nasty characters, but never in a million years did I think that she'd endure so much, go to ultimate extremes for me. Not only did she get tortured on my behalf, but she kept on fighting after that. Why did she do it? Because to her I was family, a cause she would fight to the death for. And why? Because I'd shown her kindness, treated her as an equal. At least that's what she told me when we landed in Nashville. Now that's a miracle.

Speaking of miracle, how about my dad? How had he made it to Seoul and saved my neck?

Remember what I said about tatters? It was like the old him came back when there was an emergency, and that alarm had been set when Avery visited my father and told him everything. How was she to know that dad would understand, would do something about it? Then again, this is Avery we're talking about.

They flew to Korea together on little more than faith.

Impossible.

That's what I'd thought. But it had happened anyway. Sure, Sam had helped when Avery and my father stepped into his store hours before saving my tail. How was Sam to know?

To him, dad was The Admiral. I hadn't told Sam about dad's deterioration and neither did Avery. When The Admiral asked for a weapon and ammunition, Sam gave it to him, no questions asked.

And when The Admiral had asked Sam where I was, Sam told him. According to Avery, not minutes after that, my father had disappeared, obviously heading straight into the maelstrom.

Perfect timing? Karma? Fate? Luck? All the above?

Like I said, the seeds of the future had been sown years before. The first domino toppled by the breeze of my walking past it.

When my father had hounded me into letting my kids go freely, I relented. They went to Tokyo and our lives were forever changed. The Admiral blamed himself. He'd tried to help. He'd called every friend he had left. Nothing worked, and he blamed himself again. Another domino toppled, and dad's mind began to fail.

Why am I telling you all this? Why is it important?

I want you to fully grasp how I came out of the other end of the rabbit hole. If I began this tale with revenge, I'll end it with rebirth, a new chance at life. Let me tell you how things ended.

ONE WEEK AFTER THE MESS IN KOREA

The old farmhouse needed work, and lots of it. One whole side had all but rotted away. It took me the better part of a day just to get the crumbling planks removed. The physical exertion felt good, and the sweat that poured from my body seemed to cleanse the putrescence that Shultz's gang had pumped into me.

A bell rang from the front porch.

"I'll be right there," I called out, hauling the second to last siding board away. I wiped the sweat from my brow. The bell rang again. "I said, I'm coming!"

The lawn was the next project, and I had to walk to the front through hip-deep scrub. The wild had done its best to reclaim the Greer homestead. But I had the rest of my life to beat it back.

The bell rang again. Maybe fixing the damn thing hadn't been the best idea.

I made it to the front yard before the bell could be rung again. Dad was sitting in his new rocker, bell rope in hand.

"I said I was coming, Dad."

"I like the bell," he said, not really to me. Just an observation. I don't want you to think that he went through some miraculous transformation. He still had his lucid moments, but most of the time, he was still lost.

"Are you ready for some lunch?" I asked.

"I want breakfast," he said, not grouchily, but almost as petulant as a child. "Is Avery still here?"

The old coot remembered her name more often than he did mine.

"She'll be back before dinner."

"That's good. I like her."

"I know, Dad," I said, taking the rope from his hand and laying the empty shotgun in it instead. Since moving back to the farm a week before, I'd found that there was something soothing about a weapon in my father's hands. Like a favorite blanket for a child, the touch of cold steel and a composite stock mellowed The Admiral more than my words ever could. "You want pancakes or French toast?"

"French toast, but don't make it so soft this time."

I never undercooked his French toast. That was something my mother had done, a trick she'd learned in France. A lingering memory that still tickled dad's senses. One of the tatters. No need for me to say anything.

The inside of the sprawling home was still a wreck, battered boxes intermingling with new furniture Avery had helped me order. She moved into the upstairs loft. It was the only room that was close to livable, a virtual suite. I stayed in the master bedroom while dad claimed the bedroom overlooking the fields in the back. The part-time nurse's room was right next door to his.

We'd settled into a sort of routine. After securing some of the world's best surveillance for our thousand-ish acres, I took on the repair duties while Avery made the daily trip into town to buy groceries and home decor. Dad and I had our morning ritual. Every day at sunrise, the two of us would make the trek to the family cemetery. There we would tend to the gravestones and spend time with Mom, Ella, and Caleb. It was my favorite time of day.

I thought about the kids as I cracked one egg at a time in Mom's baby blue mixing bowl. I imagined Ella smiling down on us, a family once again. I saw Caleb laughing as I struggled to pry out a stubborn nail or tripped over the overgrown brush.

Being home meant being near them. I'm not talking about their graves. To me, those headstones were just markers, where my children's mortal bodies were finally lain.

No, there was something about the land, a 'feel' more than a tangible sight or smell. My kids had loved this place, and generations of Greers had gathered here to be as one. I remembered Ella skipping down the gravel drive and Caleb wading into the stream at the bottom of the hill. Memories. They no longer haunted me. They gave me strength to move forward with my life.

I was so consumed with cooking and thinking about the kids that I didn't hear the sound of male voices before it was too late. I dropped what I was doing and ran to the front door, my right hand reaching for the pistol nestled in my back waistband. How had I missed the ding of the alarm? It was impossible for anyone to get this close.

There were three men on the front steps when I arrived, two with sidearms in hand.

"Hello, Tom," Ned Baxter said, leaning heavily on a pair of metal crutches. His left leg was encased in a brace up to his hip.

I stared at the dead man, my grip tightening on my pistol.

"What are you doing here?" I asked, taking in the two strangers. They were young, at least compared to me. Probably mid to late thirties. Both had the look of serious men, although neither gave off any unease. But they had those eyes, eyes of men that had been to war and seen the worst of the world.

"I never got to explain—" he began.

"I think you should leave," I said, opening the screen door and stepping out onto the stoop.

"Tom, we're here to help. Just let me—"

This time it wasn't me who interrupted, it was my dad.

"I know you," he said, pointing to the guy with the short brown hair and confident grin.

"You knew my father, sir," the man said, taking another step up closer to Dad.

"Don't take another step," I said, raising my weapon so that the stranger clearly understood my intent.

Now something interesting happened. The stranger didn't back down. He didn't even flinch. He just stared at me with cold calculation. I was being dissected, as if he was calculating how quickly he could take me down.

But then he smiled and said, "Let me just have a word with your father and then you can kill me. Deal?" He turned back to Dad. "Admiral, my father was Colonel Calvin Stokes."

Dad's face brightened. His gruff voice rushed out of him. "That's right! Stokes! He was one tough son of a bitch. There was this one time..." his voice trailed off, his mind seeking. "Well, I can't remember exactly, but I told your dad he should've been a SEAL."

"Yes, sir, he told me that too."

Dad rocked forward and back, maybe remembering, maybe just enjoying a moment of clarity.

Our visitor turned to me. His friend, a guy with a blond ponytail and an easy manner, hadn't moved. Something about him radiated calm. I lowered my weapon.

"My name's Cal Stokes," the first man said, not offering his hand. "The guy behind me is Daniel Briggs."

Briggs. Something about the name...

Stokes noticed the tremor of recognition.

"You remember a sniper by the name of Snake Eyes?" Stokes asked.

The flashes of old memory came storming back. Friends gone. The ambush. Too many dead. One survivor. A single sniper who'd killed hundreds to save our SEAL brethren.

"*You're* Snake Eyes?" I asked the blond stranger.

He nodded. No pride. Just affirmation.

I shook off my wonder and composed myself.

"Look, I'm glad you stopped by, but I've got a lot to get done. Can we get to the point?"

Stokes looked back at Baxter.

"Should I assume that you're less than thrilled to see our pal Ned?" he asked me.

"Probably."

"Would it help if I told you that he was working with us, that none of us knew you were even in the picture until Schultz got his hands on you?"

"That still doesn't explain why Neddy boy is there," I said.

"I've been undercover for three years," Baxter explained. "Only two people at the Bureau know what I'm doing, but they can't get involved. Cal's company is my only support."

"Your company?" I asked Stokes.

"We'll get to that later. Right now, you're the one we need to talk about."

I didn't like the way Stokes said it, like he was in charge. I was about to tell him how I deal with cocky upstarts, but Briggs stepped in.

"Your kids," said the stoic man, "do you miss them?"

For some reason, I couldn't rail at this man. It was something I couldn't grasp, that solidity. I'd never before experienced the profoundness of one man's presence.

"Of course I miss them," I said quietly.

"And you were so close."

I felt the emotion coming now, the welling of tears. Before I could reply, I felt my father's hand engulf mine, strong and calming.

He looked up at me. "We should listen to him, for the kids."

I looked between Dad and Briggs. What was happening?

My eyes met Briggs. "What do you want from me?"

Briggs smiled. "It's what you want from us, Tom."

I shook my head, not understanding. It took a beat, and then another before I understood.

They all stared at me. Dad. Baxter. Stokes. Briggs.

One deed left unfinished.

"You want to help me find her," I said. "Target Number Seven."

Briggs nodded. There was that look in his eye that told me that I would no longer fight this battle alone.

I reached out my hand and Briggs took it, still smiling. I couldn't help returning the sentiment. These men were my kind of people, men of action, men with ideals and morals. Men with courage and loyalty. Who was I to say no? It wasn't just the universe that had made the decision, it was my father who stared up at us expectantly.

I let go of Briggs's hand and looked at Stokes.

"Tell me what you had in mind," I said, eager to see which way the dominos would fall now.

His face went serious. "There's more, Tom."

"I know. More targets before we get to the last. I'm in it for the long haul."

I'll never forget the next ten seconds for as long as I live.

This stranger, this Cal Stokes, stepped closer, paused, stared dead into my eyes and said, "They're alive, Tom."

"Who?"

This he said in a voice just above a whisper. I felt every syllable.

"Your kids, Tom. They're alive, and we're going to help you find them."

+++++

Thank you so much for reading. I hope you enjoyed the story as much as I loved writing it.

If you did like it, could you do me a huge favor and take a minute to leave a review on Amazon? Even the short ones add to the success of my novels, and let me keep writing...

DON'T FORGET! Get a FREE copy of *Adrift*, the first book in the Daniel Briggs spinoff, just for subscribing at http://CG-Cooper.com

ALSO BY C. G. COOPER

Broken

Tested

The Spy In Residence Novels

What Lies Hidden

The Alex Knight Novels

Breakout

The Stars & Spies Series:

Backdrop

The Patriot Protocol Series:

The Patriot Protocol

The Chronicles of Benjamin Dragon:

Benjamin Dragon – Awakening

Benjamin Dragon – Legacy

Benjamin Dragon - Genesis

Made in the USA
San Bernardino, CA
10 March 2020